TRAIL OF THE HEART

A TALE OF TRUE LOVE DISCOVERED ONE STEP AT A TIME.

KATHLEEN PENDOLEY

Copyright © 2021 Kathleen Pendoley kathleenpendoley.com

All rights reserved.

No part of this book may be reproduced in any form or by any electronic or mechanical means, including information storage and retrieval systems, without written permission from the author, except for the use of brief quotations in a book review.

All characters appearing in this work are fictitious. Featured scenarios and events are merely figments of the author's imagination or used in said manner. Any resemblance to real persons, living or dead, is purely coincidental.

E-book design by Fat Cat Design

E-book ISBN 978-1-7371403-0-6

Paperback ISBN 978-1-7371403-2-0

ALSO BY KATHLEEN PENDOLEY

Confidence Quest - Sequel to *Trail of the Heart*

Bryant Brothers Novella Series

Beachy Keen Book 1

The Cake Maker's Dog Book 2

Glitter and Grief Book 3

A Nautical Twist Book 4

For Emma, my heart

1

JORDAN

The last mile before a zero, known as a day of rest to those off-trail, is always the most grueling. Of course, I trip on a thick root partially buried in the packed dirt. After a clumsy jig to save me from a fall, instead, I face-plant into a puddle. *Ugh! Hiking isn't for sissies.* I wipe the muck away with a bandana. So close to civilization, I can almost taste the thrills: buckets of coffee, a big, nutrient-packed salad, and deep sleep, in any order and copious amounts.

"Are you going to come and meet my host?" I ask my snuggle bunny. Everyone on the trail has a nickname. He prefers Edge. As in a life lived on the razor's edge, which is not about the two thousand mile trek we've found ourselves wayfaring.

"Naw. I ain't got time for that."

I smirk. Both of us have nothing but time. It's one of the few luxuries we've been able to take with us.

"Okay. But from what I hear, you're missing out."

He ignores me.

We reach a fork in the road. It should only be about fifteen more minutes to the parking lot. My feet are soggy, and they ache unbearably. I can almost hear the new kicks waiting for me call out, beckoning with their cushioned support.

"This is where I get off."

"Okay. I'll miss you, you know." I silently mime the response I know is coming.

"No, you won't. See ya."

"Wouldn't wanna be ya," I say to his back.

"No shit, Sherlock." Not my trail name.

I want to correct him, but he's gone, just like that. The dense green foliage camouflages Edge until the next bend erases the sound of his footfalls. Somehow the landscape allows him to come and go like a wisp. No easy feat for a man well over two hundred pounds.

I spend the rest of my fifteen-mile hike day reflecting on how perfect our flow together has become. When I need him, somehow, he is not far behind. Likewise, when I'm full up of people-time (admittedly, my threshold is low), something separates us. Kismet? Karma? I don't know, certainly some sort of universal kindness.

I spy asphalt ahead and feel tears tickle my eyelids. I live for this hike, but boy, do I love the breaks too.

Thrilled to see a black SUV waiting in the dirt lot, I quicken my pace. A tall, dark-haired man exits the driver's side and waves. I wave in response and call out, "Thank you so much for hosting me." I'm breathless from hurrying and nerves. No matter that I've learned to hitchhike. Forget that we know each other through mutual friends. I still get bat-like butterflies when getting into a car with a man I don't know. I guess you could chalk it up to being a woman in a less-than-perfectly balanced world.

The side door opens with the push of a button, and I toss my trekking poles and backpack inside. I warn him, "I'd hug you, but I stink. You'll want to put the windows down." I jump in the passenger seat and push the button to roll my side down. I'm never aware of my own stench until I'm in an enclosed space. It's rank.

Climbing into the driver's side, he's in the middle of saying, "No. It's fine," when he grimaces, head reeling back from the invisible intruder.

"It's okay. I'm well aware. You go five days without a shower. See what happens." I heckle him because it's what I do.

I can tell right away he has a good sense of humor when he responds, "You have an honest face. I believe you."

The sunburst lines around his eyes crinkle as he flashes me a dazzling white smile. He's a good-looking guy. Some salt in his pepper hair, but he's lean and fit. He looks good in khakis and a white polo shirt as he navigates the vehicle from the parking lot and down the road.

I thank him again for his hospitality.

He shakes his head. "Think nothing of it. Jonathan and I go way back, and Kim is amazing."

"Isn't she the best?" Kim is my friend who married his friend, whose sink blew up, which is why Adam is letting me crash at his place.

"She is. And how about Liam?"

"Ridiculous! Most perfect child ever. I told them when they got pregnant that they were a walking advertisement for eugenics."

He bursts out laughing. "Not the most PC compliment."

Feigning shock, I say, "No? Huh." I sit thoughtfully for a moment and decide not to share my other opinions about his friend. We get along for Kim's sake, but the guy is too handsy by half if you ask me.

I keep things light. "Do you think it was bad to suggest Liam was a parasite when Kim was pregnant and could only stomach carbs when she needed protein?"

Laughing uproariously, he wipes at his eyes. "You didn't."

"I did. And I stand by it. A fetus will get its needs met no matter the cost to the host."

"You called Kim a host? Like in *Alien*?"

"Yes! Now you're getting it. See? Perfectly appropriate in all situations. That's me."

"Well, Me, it's nice to meet you."

"Same. You can call me Jordan Roberts."

"Adam Beck."

For the next twenty miles, Adam points out the local sights. I keep peeking to get a feel of his personality. I don't think he was offended. Either way, I like him. I imagine our time together will be fun.

"Nice place," I tell Adam as he swings into his driveway, the edges lined with flowering trees past their prime. The words "pretty" and "orderly" come to mind. The grid pattern on the freshly cut lawn shows the expertise of the mower. Two massive planters accent the front door with a riot of color while perfectly cultivated perennial beds surround the house's perimeter and picket fence.

"Thanks. I had it custom built."

"Your design?"

"Not quite. Lots of my ideas, but an architect put it all together."

We pull into his three-car garage, where the only other vehicle is an older pickup. Adam sure is neat. Not a garden tool leans against a wall. Instead, each one is hung up and lined neatly in a row. His workbench is spotless, with even the small table saw free from dust of any kind.

Impossible, but I feel I've become even dirtier since leaving the trail. I suppose when a garage floor is cleaner than your skin, it would be normal to get the impression. Wanting to be fresh for Adam and his home, I point and ask, "Are those mine?" Three clearly re-used brown boxes slump limply in the corner. I don't always need what's inside when they arrive at a particular post office near the trail. That I've bumped them forward a time or two is plain to see.

"I wasn't sure if I should bring them inside or not. Flammables and stuff."

"No flammables."

"I don't know much about camping." He shrugs.

"I could teach you," I offer. "Anytime you want to meet me on the trail, just say so. You host me, and I'll hostess you."

"No, thanks. I'm good. I don't think I'm the camping type."

He doesn't look it in his neatly pressed pants and expensive leather loafers, but who knows? Nature has a way of waking you up from the inside. "Don't knock it 'til you try it," I rejoin.

"Do you want me to carry them to your room?"

I sense he wishes to get off the topic at hand—to each his own. He holds my backpack out at arm's length. I take it as a kindness to his olfactory senses.

"Naw. Right here will work. Is that trash?" I point to the plastic barrel using my keen observational skills.

"Yes."

"It'll be easier to unpack here then. Half this stuff is gonzo. It's a halfway-through-the-journey treat I planned just for me. I can't tell you how much I've been looking forward to this moment." I begin unzipping zippers and tossing my most worn and now rendered useless items into the trash can as I speak. "Do you have a box cutter or scissors?" I tend to go really liberal on the packing tape. It's a pain to open, but better than someone rifling through your stuff. Sadly, it happens to the luckiest of hikers.

He hands me both, and I tear into the boxes. There they are! My pride and joy—the new trail runners. I hug them close to my face and breathe in the rich leather smell. My feet relax already, knowing they will be ensconced in their supple sturdiness before long. I keep them cradled in the crook of my elbow and slip into a pair of sandals. I wiggle my abused toes and relish in the freedom.

"Uh, I don't want to interrupt your moment, but do you need me to help with anything?"

I put the shoes down quickly in a vain attempt to look normal. Too late. Adam has a strange look on his face. I don't think he has ever bonded with a shoe, a classic symptom of being a straight male.

"No. I'm good. Once I have a handle on this, I'll come in and shower." Touching his forearm, I repeat, "Thank you." You can't recognize kindness enough, in my opinion.

"Sure. I'll be right in the kitchen if you need anything." He's breathing through his mouth like his adenoids are swollen. The scent of the trail is not for everybody.

Before I hear the door snick to closed, I have my first layer off. Ahh, sweet liberation! I throw away my torn raincoat, duct tape on more seams than not. The upgrade I spent boatloads on should see me through until the end of my trek. I toss in my old trail runners after giving them a distant hug of gratitude. They served me well these past weeks. Into the barrel goes my trash, wrappers, Band-aids, TP, all of it gone. I feel lighter. Out with the old in with the new. I wrap my naked self in a towel, grab what's left, and look for the kitchen.

2

ADAM

What have I gotten myself into by agreeing to let Jordan stay for a few days? When a friend asks a favor, you say yes, right? So why was it all feeling so wrong then?

Jordan is sweet and certainly is polite, but man, the stench is overwhelming. I don't have a weak stomach, but that was a tough drive. I hope it doesn't linger in her stuff the way it does in the Mercedes. I'll keep the windows rolled down and make a mental note about taking the trash bin out onto the driveway. It'll be fine there until pickup. I don't want any waft finding its way into my ductwork.

I prep the ingredients for dinner. Jonathan says she's not shy around food, and I hope I bought enough. There is something wild about her long, willowy panther-like frame. I suspect she eats like one of the animals she's been colluding with out there in the woods.

She's pretty quiet, too, stealthy. I smell her before I see her standing by the kitchen island, arms filled with all kinds of junk. The towel Jordan wrapped herself in is distracting. It makes a man forget how badly she smells. Almost.

"Ready to see your room?"

"Can I start some laundry first?"

"Yes," I tell her, probably more emphatically than necessary. But this is good news.

She shoves everything, backpack included, into the washer. She moves with an efficiency that explains how she finished going through everything so quickly.

"There. Now, does that room have a shower?"

"You bet. Come this way." Maybe I was too harsh in thinking she's part animal. Although birds bathe and cats are self-cleaning, so...

Whoa! I notice the towel is smaller than I thought as I follow her up the stairs. Not such a bad thing. I clear my throat, which suddenly seems congested. "It should be stocked with everything you need."

"Oh, thanks." She turns and accidentally gives me another quick flash of flesh. "Whoops! Sorry. I don't mean to overshare." She laughs at her own joke.

Cute.

"This room is gorgeous! I feel like a princess." Jordan turns in a complete circle as she takes in the space, keeping her towel intact with a fist. "This green comforter is as pretty as a pine tree with fresh spring buds."

I grin as if in agreement when I have no idea what she's referencing. I'm not in the habit of inspecting any tree species up close.

The queen-size bed with an upholstered headboard attached to the wall takes up one side of the room, while two sets of sliding glass doors are opposite, opening to a balcony overlooking the inground pool. To the left, a wide mahogany dresser offsets a small reading space with two wingback chairs and a coffee table.

"Glad you like it." Before leading her to the bathroom, I show her all the bells and whistles: light switches, extra bedding, and drawers.

"This is huge too!"

Her eyes widen as she takes it all in. It is a pleasing room with its claw-footed tub, separate shower with numerous heads, and a water closet with a private door. She faces me, beaming.

"This is amazing, Adam. I'll never be able to thank you enough. I can't describe what it's like to go without the luxuries of life and then have every single one of them laid before you. It's beautiful. Thank you."

Afraid she might be a hugger, I swing open the linen closet door to show her the backup toiletries. "Help yourself to anything. I'll leave you to it. Oh, and dinner will be ready in about an hour, if that's okay?"

"Yes. I'm starving."

"Great. See you in a bit." I take one final peek at her shapely legs and head back to the kitchen. It's going to be a long few days.

🍯

Jordan

The bedroom Adam left me in feels palatial, and not only because I've gotten used to sleeping in a tent. The entire house is the same way. The kitchen all but echoes with its cathedral ceilings, marble counters, and open floor plan leading into the casual living room. I imagine the more formal rooms will be at least as grand and find myself looking forward to a tour.

Taking full advantage of my accommodations, I stand in the shower stall, with multiple jets on all sides, to wash off the worst of my grime while the bathtub fills with hot water and bubbles. I slide in slowly when it's about to overflow, savoring every molecule. Another contrast strikes me: stinky to sparkly. So worth getting dirty, if only to get this squeaky clean.

Shocking to think that just last night, I curled up next to my snuggle bunny, neither of us noticing or caring about our stench. I smile, remembering how long it took us to get to that point—in trail time, not in actual time.

We began on the same day, about a week before most northbound thru-hikers would be preparing to depart from Springer Mountain in Georgia. The extended forecast was calling for a warmer than average spring. I was raring to go, and Edge was just Edge. He hikes. That's what he does. As he put it, "I'm going to be in the woods, might as well be this woods." That was the sum total of our dialogue after my first attempt to make a friend.

He avoided me like the plague, but we had this way of running into one another from the start. I'd gab and try to get him to engage. Edge would sit silently, continuing with whatever he was doing until he was finished. Then he would gather his things and leave, no nice talking to you, no goodbye, nothing.

Edge took a tumble one particular Sunday, cutting a gash in his hairline right over his temple. Moments later, I came upon him, still on the ground with blood pouring from the wound. After an argument over how he didn't need help, he finally relented when I threatened to take his pack and go call for an ambulance. I had to cut a large section of hair, dreadful for a mountain man like him. After washing and disinfecting the area, I used super glue to seal it up.

Left without an excuse to fend me off any longer, he began hiking willingly with me, tuning into my tales of woe, the things that had brought me to the path. My divorce, my parents' early deaths, and my estrangement from my stepsister, I laid it all out.

Eventually, he began to open up himself. Initially, tiny hints like a trail of breadcrumbs. Then, like a spigot turned to full blast, came a torrent. For days we would walk, and he would tell the ghastly details of his experience, putting my own to shame.

Although I would never tell this part to a soul, he cried like a broken-hearted little boy once he let it all out. I could hear him in his tent and couldn't bear it. So I crawled in and held him, allowing him the space to let it all go. Though not sexual in any way, we fell in a sort of love that night and have been close ever since.

If need be, I can always explain our unique relationship by describing our second night together when a storm struck. It was a terrible night. We zipped our bags together and held each other close. Barely sleeping, we talked to overcome the gripping fear of what may happen. He shared more of his story, graphic medical details, and harrowing days spent arguing in court. I shared my inability to conceive, the physical ailment that upended my own life. We grew even closer that night, bonding through our pain and our commitment to press on regardless, not just on the hike but in life.

Enough of that! My thoughts return to the present moment. I soak until the water becomes tepid and my muscles torpid. My grumbling belly encourages me from within. I can smell the garlic, cheese, and tomato sauce and find I can't dry off fast enough.

3

JORDAN

Adam hands me a glass of wine right as I arrive and motions to a platter filled with cheese, crackers, and black olives. Before taking a sip, I build myself three little sandwiches, eating each in rapid succession. Swallowing it all down with the chardonnay, I find it tastes like the kitchen looks: crisp, clean, and bright.

"Tasty."

"1981 was a good year for Spanish wine."

"Ah, a connoisseur." Is he trying to intimidate me or impress me? Or is he a total douche? I suppose that's also a possibility. He is Jonathan's friend, after all.

"I read it on the shelf label."

The wine almost comes out of my nose.

"Gotcha."

"You did. I like it."

"The wine?"

"And that you played me." I take another slug to wash the choking away. "Do we have time for a tour?"

He finishes wiping down what appears to be an already spotless counter. "Sure."

I grab the tray of food. Adam gives me a side-eye, and I feel the need to explain myself. "Emergencies can happen anytime, anywhere. Preparation is the antidote."

As with the shoes, he doesn't understand but silently leads the way.

❧

Adam

I've got to hand it to the woman; she cleans up well. Dressed in a body-skimming sundress, Jordan now smells of strawberries. Her dark chocolate-colored hair is long and looks soft as silk. Even her feet, the wild one goes barefoot, are dainty and feminine. Such a far cry from the dirty, disheveled mess I met a few short hours ago. Bonus: that great sense of humor. She can dish it out and take it, two admirable qualities.

Jordan seems to be enjoying the tour, complimenting every room with a "wow" or a "beautiful," sometimes standing in silent awe. That was in the main foyer. The chandelier is striking. It had to be, hanging as it is from the thirty-foot ceiling. The ceiling itself is a masterpiece. Coffered with thick beams painted white and the paint within blue, a Grecian silhouette in a Wedgwood-style adorns every other section.

"And now the library." Taking up most of one half of the house, it is as quiet as a chapel. The only other room is my office. We'll skip that. I assume she is familiar with desks and computers.

The books on shelves from floor to ceiling cover three walls, interspersed with stained glass windows, fronted by leather chairs and mahogany tables. I watch Jordan turn slowly, taking it all in. The light from the setting sun streams color in, dancing across her pretty features. It turns her dark hair almost blue, the red of her lips deepening as though she's been thoroughly kissed.

"This is my favorite," she whispers reverently.

I snap out of my reverie. "Mine too. Help yourself. I have everything from Chaucer to Twain and King to Berg."

"Funny that you put the king of terror, pun intended, with the lady who makes the prosaic not only interesting but enviable. They're both so different and yet so similar in their ability to spin a tale. She is truly Queen to his King-ness. I always feel better for having read an Elizabeth Berg book. Like a visit with a kindly and sage aunt who gets it, you know?"

"How do you feel after reading Stephen King?"

"Terror, Adam. Sheer terror. But he leaves me wanting more. How about you? Who are your favorites here?"

"Hm. Hard to say. As far as contemporary authors, I guess Steinbeck and Cook."

"Two more contrasts. Mundane to the point of watching paint dry and medical intrigue."

"Jordan, people love Steinbeck. He's an American classic. *Of Mice and Men, The Grapes of Wrath, The Pearl.*"

"Adam, you can keep your list. I went to high school. Is it literature? Yes, that is some fine literature right there. Can the guy tell an interesting story? Weave a tale? Hold my interest? That's a triple no. On a different day, I might argue he's not contemporary either, but we can back burner that." She studies my scowling face for several seconds. "Looks like Steinbeck is a hot button issue for you."

Now she speaks the truth. If she didn't look so cute with her dimples showing as she tries to contain her laughter, I might leave her in the library and let her find her way back.

Scratch that. She probably has a pretty good sense of direction from living like a savage.

"Let's agree to disagree." I let her off easy. She is my guest, after all.

"Well, I'd rather agree that I'm right, and you have no taste, but okay, agree to disagree." As though reading my mind—great, now I'm creating puns—she follows up with, "Now lead me to the kitchen. My nose senses dinner is ready, and I'm quite lost."

"I have one more room to show you."

"Another?" Her expression is incredulous. "Do you need so many rooms?"

Chapter 3

"You have the entire East Coast. Talk about the pot calling the kettle black."

Jordan elbows me unexpectedly. The platter of hors d'oeuvres I ended up carrying so she could eat slips from my hands, spilling its scant remains on the hardwood.

"Whoops! Let me get that. She picks up the two crackers and single olive, placing them back on the tray.

For a second, I thought she was going to pop them in her mouth. I may have to go food shopping again if she keeps eating this way.

"I don't own any of the trails." She gestures up, down, and all around us. "I mean, all this square footage for one single guy. Astounding."

"Don't forget I have a visitor. She takes up some space." I noticed the sprawl as I passed by her bedroom. She's making herself comfortable, and I'm glad. How she finds anything in the chaos, though, is anyone's guess.

I open the final door, and a billow of heat greets us.

"A solarium?" Her smile is contagious. "This is my favorite, too. Can I bring a book in here?"

"Sure. I do that sometimes myself. Usually, in the winter, but anytime is good."

Small trees, miniature shrubbery, and loads of plants surround us.

"I never liked how you mostly only see your gardens when you're coming and going. I tend to angle the chairs outward towards the lawn, and the plantings are closer to the house. So, I brought the garden inside.

"I eat my breakfast here a lot. Maybe we can do that during your stay?" For some unexplained reason, I want to please this woman. Maybe it's because she makes it so easy. Everything I've shown her or offered, so far, she greets with authentic pleasure. It makes a guy feel good to be appreciated.

"I would love that."

When she turns her hazel eyes my way, I find myself wishing we were back in the library. I bet those colors would pop, reflecting the stained glass.

"Adam, this is so wonderful. Thank you." She takes me by the arm and asks, "Food now?" Her belly rumbles like an exclamation point, pushy and insistent.

4

JORDAN

Once we're seated, I begin shoveling food onto the pretty blue Delftware Adam set. Penne pasta smothered in sauce, three large meatballs, and half of the loaf of cheesy garlic bread (in my defense, he made it with a long, narrow French bread) fill up every inch of my dinner plate.

Adam doesn't move.

Curious why, I look up from my plate, with a leaf from the crisp, dressing-laden Caesar salad poking out from the side of my mouth. Then, pushing it in like a lumberjack, I ask, "What?" I haven't swallowed yet, so my question is garbled.

"Don't you say grace?"

"Why would you assume that?" I wipe my mouth clean and take a sip of water.

"Jonathan described you as kind of kumbaya about the universe and stuff." He waves his arm up toward the ceiling, making me look. I don't find God or an angel, just a stylish light fixture.

"The universe knows my heart. Can't you tell how I feel about food?" I see no point in adding my belief that Jonathan doesn't know shit about anything.

"Aggressive," he answers in a rather matter-of-fact way.

Adam really can make me laugh. "Guilty, but I also love it. I haven't yet discovered a meal or a morsel that I don't appreciate. It doesn't even have to taste very good. Most people wouldn't stomach the crap I eat on the trail for long, but I'm grateful for every calorie." I shrug. "But if you're more comfortable with the pomp, then, by all means, let's say grace." I fold my hands and close my eyes to enjoy the quaint charm of an official blessing.

Nothing happens. Peeking out from the corner of my eye, I find him staring. "What?" This time I have no food in my mouth to hinder communication.

"I don't say it, either. I was offering for you."

"Oh." Now things feel awkward. "Well, why not do it anyway? Then we can move past it. Shall I?" I may not interact with many humans on the trail, but they sure are an interesting lot when you get up close and personal.

Adam nods assent and folds his hands.

I take a deep breath and begin. "Dear Deity, man, woman, seedling, we don't know. We do know you have enabled us to fill our bellies with delicious food. Thank you."

He picks up his fork only to place it back down as I continue.

"We also know you keep us safe and cared for on this journey called life. It's a beautiful gift to simply breathe the free air, gaze upon the beautiful landscape, and tread on the solid earth. Thank you."

Now he grabs for his wine glass. He takes a quick sip, then grudgingly places it back down when he sees me frown.

"Sorry," he says. I shush him with my finger against my lips.

"You give us one another to lessen our burdens, uplift our spirits, and bring joy to our experience. Thank you."

He doesn't dare move now that I've found my groove. You call me kumbaya; you throw down a gauntlet. I'm going to give the grace to end all graces. Or something close to it.

"You give us strength and endurance and test us mercilessly, time and again. You ask for everything and will stop at nothing to get it. You knock us down, watch us struggle to get back up, and rejoice when we stumble again." I watch him through my eyelashes, fussing with his napkin and looking unsure. It's hard not to laugh, knowing this could get dark really fast.

My belly gurgles out a protest. *Okay fine.* The consensus is I should wrap it up.

"You enabled this generous man to invite me into his home, make fine food, and share his deplorable taste in novels. That is a level of trust I will honor. I vow before you to keep his dirty little secret from the rest of the world." I stop for a moment to say, "You're welcome."

He remains silent.

"In closing, 'Good bread, good meat, good gosh, let's eat!'" I finish with a flourish, lifting both fork and knife. "Was that okay?" I ask innocently.

"I don't know. I'm not religious."

"You didn't like it?"

"I'd say it was fine. Tedious and long but fine."

"You'd know," I mumble as I sprinkle my dish with Parmesan cheese.

Mmm. These meatballs are to die for, definitely worth the gratitude.

"Is that some sort of dig?" He's tucking in, so I figure he's having fun, too.

"Totally. You love Steinbeck. Hence, you love tedious and long." Before I go too far, which I suppose can happen now and again, I tell him truthfully, "This meal is delicious. The best I've had off-trail. You didn't have to go to so much trouble, but I'm so glad you did."

"You're welcome. Jonathan mentioned you liked Italian."

"Love it. It sits so nicely in your belly. Even when you overeat, it feels like a hug from inside."

He tops off both wine glasses, killing the bottle.

"Who taught you to cook, Adam?"

"Pierre Rene Labrousse."

"Pretty."

"Hardly. Pierre was your stereotypical chef. Crude, rude, gassy, and drunk most of the time."

"I thought you were a techie guy."

"I am. I took a six-month holiday in France to learn about European cuisine after I sold my first business."

"From where I'm sitting, I'd say worth it." Finally finished, I wipe my mouth vigorously with an ivory-colored napkin. Big mistake. "Sorry. Got any bleach? I can toss this in with my sheets before I go."

"Don't worry about it," he tells me graciously. "My housekeeper will take care of it."

I find myself forgetting people live differently than me, and the contrast is even starker in Adam's case.

"I'll just get it started with a good soak." I carry it and my dishes to the sink, rinsing it all in cold water. I wring out the napkin and hang it over the faucet to gather more dinnerware.

"Leave it. Lisa will be here first thing. She'll get it."

"Naw. Cleaning up is the least I can do. Plus, if my eyes aren't playing tricks, that looks like a cake, and where there's cake, there's ice cream. Doing the dishes will help things settle, and I'll have more space for dessert."

Shaking his head, he brings the rest of the utensils and joins me at the sink.

"I'll wash, you dry."

"We," he stretches the word out long, "will stack the dishwasher."

Once everything is tidy, Adam finds us another bottle of wine to go with dessert and invites me to the balcony beyond. The view is spectacular. Pastures a-plenty are dotted with dark forms that look suspiciously like cows. "Dairy farm?" I'm pretty astute.

He nods.

I knew it.

Taking a bite of my dessert, I belt out, "Oh my, yes!" The thick chocolate frosting melts on my tongue. Fat, sugar, and cocoa are in perfect heavenly balance. The next bite includes ice cream. Mixing in the vanilla bean brings it to the next level of nirvana.

He's on his feet, looking ready to fight. "What is it?" he hollers, trying to take my plate.

"No! Stop." I'm not giving this up without a court injunction.

"Are you okay? I thought you were hurt when you called out."

Chapter 4

I pat his chair, encouraging him to sit again. "Oh, no. That was my ecstasy, 'Oh my, yes.'"

He appears to be blushing at my comment in the dim light, so I change the subject. "Did you make the cake?"

"And the ice cream."

"That's it. I'm moving in."

We finish our food quietly as the evening fades into night.

※

Stars speckle the night sky in a celestial connect-the-dots. Bright for a suburban area, I try to explain to Adam what it looks like without the distraction of any electricity whatsoever.

"Truly, if you want the best star experience, you have to head out west. Arizona. Wyoming. You know, big sky country. It's not just an advertisement lure to improve tourism. It seems like you'll never reach the horizon; space goes on forever. Have you been?"

It turns out, he's a great listener. I made polite inquiries about what he does for fun and work, but even he admitted it was putting us both to sleep. He works with people, tells them what to do, makes a ton of money doing it, blah, blah, blah. It's a story anyone can fill in the blanks to. It definitely puts the "boo" in booooring.

"Only for conferences. To the hotel and back to the plane. No sightseeing."

"Oh, Adam. That's so sad. You know what they say about all work and no play."

"Yeah, I'm familiar."

"Thought so."

He gives me a friendly glare. "Please, do go on." Sarcasm frames his words.

"Well, it's stunning. I would say a must-see, even though looking up at the sky on the Appalachian Trail is a sight in itself, especially when you're on a mountaintop. Oh, it seems you could leap straight out and be safely caught, like being at a rave. It's a velvety, midnight-blue blanket, sparkling crystals included."

As we continue to look up, with me waxing poetic about my nights, a shooting star whips across the sky at warp speed.

"Wow!" I lean over and give him a big smooch on the cheek. Just as quickly, I'm back on my side, tucking my legs underneath me. I didn't expect a thrill from a cheek, but I got one. I touch my lips, believing I'll feel some residual tingling.

He seems to have experienced it, too. His fingertips stray to his cheek as he asks, "What was that for?"

"That's for luck. We saw a shooting star. You don't want it to slip away, do you?"

Not sounding swayed by my interpretation, Adam abruptly switches gears. "I don't want to keep you up. I know you must be looking forward to bed."

"Mmm. Am I ever." I moan with desire. As decadent as his dessert, a bed is going to feel sensuous in its pleasure.

Adam coughs into his fist and moves further down the bench before continuing. "I'd love to hear a few trail stories, but only if you're up for it. Otherwise, maybe over breakfast?"

He is the most considerate host and has me thinking I should be grateful that Kim burst a pipe.

"I'm up for one or two." My yawn interrupts me.

"One is good," he assures me.

"Okay. Let's see." I go through my mental Trail Tales file. "Oh. I've got just the story for you." We continue watching the night sky for more luck as I tell a tale featuring a chipmunk and a rat.

"The entire week had been brutally cold. Go figure, the day it warms up, the rain begins to fall in sheets. No rain gear, save a dwelling, was going to keep anyone dry. I kept them on for the extra layer, but I was soaked to the skin. My shoes filled with water, squelching in the mud, keeping my wool socks a soggy mess.

"Stopping was not an option as I had to make it to the next town for my mail delivery. Supplies were running low, and I needed what was in that box, plus a few things from the local store.

"Around noon, the rain stopped, and the sun came out. Not a gradual thing, more like the main valve had been shut off, blue skies,

Chapter 4

not a cloud around, and the temperature somewhere in the mid-sixties. If I weren't still drenched, I would have thought I imagined the entire thing.

"I wrung out my socks and tossed all my wet stuff onto a rock to dry, then had my first sit-down meal of the day.

"Large puddles were everywhere on the trail, one not five feet from my picnic spot. The cutest chipmunk came out from the underbrush and stopped to take a drink. I held my sandwich in midair, not wanting to spook the little guy and deny him some fresh water.

"As my heart melted, another critter came out from the opposite side of the trail. A rat! Maybe three times the size of the chipmunk, he was as stealthy as air. He grabbed my woodland friend, gave a quick shake to snap his neck, and ran off with him back into the woods.

"I sat there, the sandwich still up, paralyzed with horror. It took a good ten minutes before I could eat. Even then, I finished only to avoid wasting it. A rare thing for me to lose my appetite, but that did it.

"I mean, I understand a rat has to eat, and in nature, that's what it's all about, but he did ruin my meal. Although, to give him credit, the little chipmunk never saw it coming. There and gone in the blink of an eye."

I take my gaze off the sky and look at him. Adam is watching me too. He's still handsome, even with his face twisted in revulsion.

"Do you know the moral of the story, Adam?"

"Don't go in the woods? Animals live there."

He's dead serious, and I'm clutching my sides laughing. I'm having such fun, though it's obvious we share no common interests. We are so very different.

"No, Adam. That is not it. The moral is to get out there, live, and enjoy. It could be your last drink, so make it a good one." With that said, I stand, ready for bed.

"Are you coming?" I ask, offering a hand to help him up.

"I think I'll sit up a while longer. Goodnight, Jordan."

Unwittingly, my hand reaches out to touch his face, where I kissed him. My fingertips tingle. "Goodnight."

5

JORDAN

The sun appears to have been up well before I wake. Bright sunshine streams through the gauzy curtains, strong enough to convince me to move. The bed just feels so good underneath my normally aching back that I want to freeze-frame the moment.

Every morning on the forest floor, I wake to pain somewhere in my body, but today, nothing. Every cell feels rested and alive. Trusting the healthy vibe, I roll over and look at the clock. Yup, ten hours of uninterrupted sleep, I guess that will do it.

Incapable of thought before coffee, I grab my phone and head down to rustle some up. Maybe I'll find a piece of that cake to go with it. I salivate and quicken my pace. Rounding the corner, I see Adam in the kitchen, threateningly close to the coffee pot that looks only half full.

Forgetting my manners, I blurt out, "I thought you'd be at work."

Embarrassingly late, I realize I forgot to pack a robe for my visit. The air conditioning must be cranked up high as my nipples act as chief meteorologists, straining against my tank top's thin cotton. He's reading the forecast right from my chest. Who can blame him? They are quite the beacon.

"Sorry. I'll get dressed. Can I just have that?" I point like a child to the carafe now in his hands. "I need it so bad."

His eyes grow rounder.

Shit. Did I seriously say that out loud? I'm not myself yet. Caffeine will make it all better.

"Sure," he says after he collects himself. He pours it into a heavy mug and points to the milk and sugar. I use both and flit off to get dressed.

"You don't have to leave on my account. I want you to be comfortable." Adam offers as he busies himself, lining up the extra coffee cups in a way that suggests he's not very comfortable.

"No, that's okay. I'll be down in a bit." I scurry away to ingest the liquid manna.

ADAM

No doubt about it, the woman is going to be the death of me. The way Jordan appeared like that, all tousled hair and hardened nipples. And what did she say? Oh, yes. "I need it so bad." I thought she was making a play and damned if I wasn't going to go for it. She's lucky I picked up on her other physical cues, like staring at the coffee as she reached her greedy little hands toward the mug. Thinking of her surprise if I hadn't has me smiling. We'd be together in the bedroom she fled to, instead of me here alone, brewing another pot.

Two more days, I tell myself. You can handle it for two more days. You're not a frat boy on spring break, and she's not a woman with whom you should get involved. There. My mind is prepared and relaxed. Now to convince the rest of my body to get on board.

She's back. More clothing, though not much more. At least she's wearing a bra. Her jeans hug her every curve, and the holes are made organically through wear and tear. They look as soft as a second skin. My fists clench by my sides to stop them from testing out the fabric.

"Good morning." Jordan acts as though it's our first encounter of the day. "Mind if I get a cup?" She's filling the mug already.

"Help yourself. Are you ready to eat? I can make you an omelet or something."

"You're spoiling me. And, yes, omelet, please. Anything you've got to put inside, I'll take it."

I swallow hard, stopping the groan in my throat from escaping. I don't think Jordan even realizes what she says half the time.

"And cake. May I have some cake?"

"You can have anything you want." I'm a good host, that is all. Or so I tell myself.

"Mmm. I like the sound of that." She's right beside me. As tall as she is, Jordan all but whispers it into my eardrum.

I've got no response, so I keep my focus on the hot pan instead. "Go," I tell her, pointing to the couch on the opposite wall. "Sit and enjoy your coffee."

"You said I could have cake."

I turn to find her body a hairsbreadth from my own. With my eyes laser-focused on her full lips, I say, "Yes," breathy as an ingenue. She needs to step away before I embarrass myself further.

Her face brightens. "Thanks! Where is it?"

Where did she get the fork?

"I came prepared. All I could think about was dessert for breakfast."

"The cake's next to the fridge," I tell her without sharing what I was thinking about her first impression this morning.

After a quick stir, I pour the egg into the skillet and let it slowly cook. I busy my hands, chopping onion, pepper, and mushrooms into bite-size pieces, tossing them in after flipping the omelet. After sprinkling on a pinch of shredded cheese, it's ready to slide off the pan.

"You want juice or toast?" I ask.

Jordan sits at the table, primly covering her lap with a napkin. She seems to know that social grace, at least. And she does say thank you more than anyone I've ever met. So maybe she's not entirely animal, though I'm no longer sure whether that's a good thing.

"No, thanks. This is perfect." She places the cake to the side as I set the omelet before her. "Look at that. I can't believe how thin you got the egg. It's gorgeous."

It is. A few cheese shreds escaped, blending with the butter, the color contrasting like caramel against the egg's creamy yellow.

Speaking around her first mouthful, she says, "I thought you were working."

"I took a few days off."

"For me?"

"Yes."

"Aww. You didn't have to. It's enough that you've sheltered me."

"It's not a big deal. I often work from home anyway, so if I needed to, I could."

"Oh, good. I don't want to be intrusive or disruptive."

"You aren't." She is but not in the worst way. "We'll be gone most of the day anyway."

"Ooh!" She drops her fork and claps her hands. "Yay! I love surprises. What is it?"

"We're going to see Jonathan and Kim."

"Oh, my gosh. That's great news. I was hoping to see her. I mean, them, but I wasn't sure how. I was thinking of hitchhiking. People are usually pretty cool with us thru-hikers."

"I can drive you anywhere you need to go." I cut in, feeling protective all of a sudden. Last week, I read a story about a nightclub where a young lady tried to be responsible after a night of heavy drinking and called for a car. She never made it home.

Jordan interrupts my thought pattern, her hand clutching my arm. Her fingers are strong but surprisingly soft. Lust begins to override my fear. *Lame*. It's just a hand.

"Hey, are you okay? You looked angry for a second."

I laugh it off. "Naw. It's nothing. Anyway, we're meeting them at Tranquil Transitions."

She knocks back the rest of her coffee. "What's that?"

I hand her a pamphlet about a local day spa. "They felt terrible about bailing on you, so they booked a complete day package for you and Kim. Massage, facials, mani-pedis, whatever that is."

"Oh. My. Yes."

Not Jordan's ecstatic version of "Oh my, yes!" it still sounds happy, to be sure.

"I can't believe it. This is too much." Tears well in her eyes. "I mean, I cannot tell you how heavenly using a private bath is. That is more than enough to make this gal happy. But no. There's this." She spreads her arms about her. "And this." She spears a chunk of omelet and chews it up. "And now this. I love being pampered. This is the best day of my life. "So, what are you and Jonathan going to do?" She often says his name peculiarly. I briefly wonder why before answering her question.

"We're taking Liam to the lake until his grandmother comes to watch him. Then we'll meet with you ladies for dinner right after. Jonathan got reservations at a fancy Italian place."

When she starts asking questions about hair and oils, I wave her concerns away. "They'll do your hair and all that beforehand. What do you think?"

"Am I dead?" She thrusts her arm out. "Pinch me."

"No. And you're not dead."

"Pinch me, or I'll never believe it."

I need to remember her strangeness if I run into her semi-clad again. I pinch her.

With awe in her voice, she says, "This is real." She jumps to stand, clearing her plates. "I've got to pack a bag. When do we leave?"

"Two hours."

"Phew, that was close. I'll have more coffee instead." Jordan glides to the coffee maker, holding up the pot. "More?"

I nod my assent. Jordan may be odd, but I'm finding I rather like odd.

6

JORDAN

While nursing our coffees, the conversation makes the time go by quickly.

Swapping stories from our pasts, Adam is finishing up a rather engaging anecdote from boyhood.

"Everybody knows about the 'Be home before the streetlights go on period,' and I remember the paradigm vaguely. But, from an onlookers vantage point, I guess you could say.

"My older sister, Nora, was part of the neighborhood group. Anytime they congregated, they'd play kickball, dodgeball, baseball." He ticks them off on his fingers. "When it got dark, it was flashlight tag or chasing fireflies. Every summer night brought all the kids outside after dinner. I mean, it just doesn't seem that long ago when everyone ate the evening meal at the same time. Most of the group could be out until the streetlights came on, others a bit longer. Those were the lucky ones.

"Me, not so much. I had to go home and straight to bed before anyone else. My sister didn't wear a watch but somehow always knew when it was six-thirty. She would swear she heard my mother call. Half the time, my mother was sauced, the other half hungover, so I don't think she ever looked for me at all."

I wrap him in a brief hug to ease his pain and fill his coffee one last time. "Mind if I grab a croissant?"

"Help yourself."

A light seems to be dawning inside his head while the outside of the pastry flakes onto my lap. The part I get in my mouth melts like butter. I moan my pleasure, too busy eating to compliment him verbally on another homemade creation. I jump up to grab another before gesturing for him to continue.

"Now that we're discussing it, I think my sister made the whole damn thing up. I probably didn't even have a curfew. I know she was always making goo-goo eyes at Tim Mathews and didn't want me tagging along.

"The year I was old enough to hang out with them past Nora's trumped-up curfew, they all started middle school and organized sports. The entire dynamic changed. Not just in my neighborhood but everywhere. Parents got scared, kids got micromanaged, and there hardly seems to be a demarcation line between them these days." He pauses to sip his coffee. "I don't know. I suppose I'm a jaded old man."

"Not so old," I tell him for both our benefits. I'm thirty-seven, and he can't have that many years on me.

"How about you? Siblings? A fun neighborhood? Any Tim Mathews lurking in your past?"

I give him a half snort around the dregs of my coffee. "Hardly. I lived with my mom in an apartment building after my parents divorced. There weren't too many kids. Even if there had been, there was no open space to play. A rusty, weed-filled playground was on the next corner, and I went there sometimes. Not super fun, more for a change of scenery. I got a lot of cuts and scrapes playing on the metal swing set. It's a wonder I never got tetanus."

"Sounds lonely," he tells me. "I can picture how cute you must have looked in pigtails."

"Thanks. I think I was an adorable kid now that you mention it."

Adam acts as though he's interested in what I have to say, so different from how my ex-husband Brett behaved in similar situations, and I find myself sharing more than I expected. "A lot of days I was very lonely. But I also learned how to be alone, which is a skill no one can ever take away from you."

"Part of why you're doing this, maybe?"

"Maybe. Not exclusively."

"Intriguing." He raises one eyebrow. I'm not sure if it's because of what I said or the fact that I just finished the rest of the croissants. "Go on."

"Everything and nothing."

"Specific," he mocks lightly.

"I got to a point where I couldn't anymore. I couldn't function the way I was. I couldn't think straight. I felt like I couldn't breathe, you know?" The slightest tickle of a tear pricks my eyes. But I'm not crying in front of a stranger. This break is supposed to be pleasant, and I refuse to let my negative experience override it. My goal is to wrap it up quickly. "My life kind of imploded around me, leaving me with few options and little in the way of ideas.

"But throughout my life, I've always hiked any chance I could get. Even when I worked in the city, I always found an oasis of green. I would spend all my free time there, the same as I did at that dilapidated playground as a child. It might not have been big or fancy, but it was outside. Nature made sense to me. It still does. So I read a ton of books, watched a few videos, and met my mentor, Jenna. She's a triple crown."

"A what?"

"It means she's hiked the AT, the PCT, and CDT."

He still looks at me as though I've spoken Greek. My trail-speak has to be translated as though it were a different language.

"The Appalachian Trail, the Pacific Crest Trail, and the Continental Divide Trail. Jenna has hiked them all. She's amazing and so inspirational.

"So, I decided the trail was where I belonged, at least for a time. It was an answer to my questions. Not the one I expected, mind you, but I've learned not to look an answer from my higher source in the mouth."

I'm unwilling to go down the tale of woe road and prepare to bolt.

"Hey, thanks for the convo. It was fun walking down memory lane, but I should get to packing for the spa." I collect our dishes and plates.

Again, he insists I leave everything.

"Seriously, Lisa won't have anything to do. She tells me all the time she'll stop coming if I don't need her, even though I know she needs the money."

"Why would she tell you that?"

"Pride. Her husband bailed on her and their two boys a year ago. Her oldest has Down syndrome, so she already has a lot on her plate. Lisa is older than I am, and I hate to think of her getting a second job or a third because I don't have enough here for her to do. Frankly, with just me, there isn't. I try to be messy, but..." He trails off. I wonder if he's seen the state of my bedroom. Lisa will have a field day in there if I don't hoof it upstairs and straighten my mess.

"You don't have to convince me, Adam. I've seen your garage." Before I head upstairs, I squeeze his shoulder. "That's a kind thing to do. More people should be like you."

"It's nothing."

"I don't believe you, but okay," I sing-song the taunt as I climb the stairs.

Adam

I let Jordan have her delusion. I have so much bad karma to work off that almost nothing I do for others will ever be enough to count as kindness.

7

JORDAN

I hug Kim tightly, deftly avoid Jonathan's waiting arms, and reach for baby Liam. "Gimme, gimme." He gurgles and drools and giggles, and I'm head over heels. "Oh, you squishy-ishy dumpling baby." His pudgy arms wrap tight around my neck, and I feel his milky breath against my ear. "Can I keep him? Please?"

"Jonathan, get the baby." Kim smiles adoringly at her son as she destroys my hope.

"No." I turn away from his grab. "I said, please."

Liam giggles at the spinning, so I take another go around. More giggles. The sound is sweeter than anything I've ever heard, and I want to keep moving, so it never stops.

Kim has other plans as she steps into our space and expertly removes the chubby cherub from my arms. With both hands, he grabs her necklace and pops the pendant right into his mouth. "He's hungry."

"Fine. I can sympathize with that. I'm the last person to get in the way of a good meal." I kiss his still bald head. "See you later, Liam." I coo until he's heading away with his dad and my patron.

"You made one adorable baby, my friend." We watch until the three males disappear from view.

"Don't I know it." Love softens her already attractive features.

I'm jealous, but in the best way. Kim found her place. I thought I had, but no, I'm still seeking.

"Hey, Jordan, how is Adam treating you?" Kim needs to whisper now that we're in the dimly lit confines of the spa. Light music, Chopin accompanied by waves, I believe, and a lovely lavender/vanilla scent beckons us forward to the hostess station.

"He's fun. Thanks for finding me housing on such short notice."

"Well, it was our fault, not yours. It was the least we could do. And sorry, did you say fun? Adam is the most serious guy on earth."

I don't even know how to respond, so I don't. I feel like I've been laughing since I hopped in Adam's car. Maybe it's our proximity that leaves him less guarded around me.

"Good afternoon, ladies."

"Good afternoon," we parrot at the same time. I smack Kim on the ribs and say, "Coke." A free drink for me at dinner, and it won't be a soda.

"Grow up," she whispers as Hope leads us to the changing room.

We catch up on the details of our lives. Kim tells mommy stories from the heart. I fill her in on trail stories of random acts of kindness. Neither of us would be happy with the other's life. Of course, my problem is Jonathan, though I would jump through hoops of fire to have a baby like Liam. Kim couldn't enjoy the trail because of her mortal fear of anything unpredictable. And spiders. She really hates spiders.

Jasmine interrupts to take Kim inside first. Soon after, Star leads me to my room. I contemplate the possibility that everyone here has one name for work and another for the world beyond these large oak doors, just like us thru-hikers. But when Star begins to work my overused muscles, I cease to care.

≈

Rubbed, buffed, and beautified, we stroll out to the lobby. Our men wait for us, looking uncomfortable surrounded by scented tea lights, tasteful throw pillows, and chandeliers festooned with crystals.

Chapter 7

Nope! Wrong word. Not our men. I correct myself. *Kim's husband and my host.* I bond too quickly, or so my last therapist thought. Perhaps true, but not in this case. I won't be here long enough to connect. Adam is friendly and funny, and that's where it begins and ends.

So why am I worrying my brain space over this line of thought? Shaking my head to return to the present moment, I wave as we get closer.

Adam looks at me strangely.

"Hi," I greet him casually, ignoring Kim and Jonathan as they canoodle.

Adam simply stares as I make another vain attempt at communicating. "How was your day?"

"Fine." The single word is all he shares.

I fill in the void by telling him about mine. "Today was great. I feel so loose and free, like anything could happen. Starving too. What else is new, right?" Maybe some humor will help him engage.

"Sure."

And maybe not. It could be Kim is right, and I've read him all wrong. He seems serious now, so different from how he acts when we're alone.

"You two ready?" Jonathan asks as he helps Kim slip into her heels. She only had the sneakers she came with, and they clash horribly with her off-the-shoulder, red flamenco-style dress.

You would never imagine the woman had a baby less than a year ago. Hard work and excellent genes will do it every time. At least that's what she tells me. I'm not able to conceive, so I'll never know. Plus, I suspect my genes might be a tad wonky.

"Definitely," I answer for us all.

Adam and I follow them to the restaurant silently in his SUV.

꽃

ADAM

I did not sign up for this. Jordan talks of contrast in her life, and here she sits, some sort of chameleon. I wouldn't have recognized her when she walked out if she hadn't been with Kim. Her hair, no longer tousled and wild, is piled high on her head with loose strands curling down to touch her shoulders, bare save two thin straps. Her white dress makes her look part seductress/part virgin, both enticing in their own way. Wearing no jewelry, she kept all the sparkle for her feet, glittery gold toes in sequined high heels. Sex on a stick, she is no longer a wild forest tramp but a sultry siren.

On the outside, my life looks full of indulgence. I have the house, the car, the prestigious job, but it's all from "before." Before I surrendered the right to feel joy, love, or any high emotion. I haven't felt so much as a niggle for years and don't appreciate the test now. She's not even my type, so why have I lost my ability to speak? I could barely give one-word answers to her mundane questions.

Jordan no longer knows how to act, evidenced when I feel her eyes dart in my direction. She just opened her mouth to say something and changed her mind, turning on the radio instead. She hits buttons until stopping on a classical station. Violins fill the void, leaving the atmosphere marginally more comfortable.

Jordan

The waiter serves our meals as I finish telling my favorite wildlife story of the hike so far. "And there it was, a black bear, just like the sign warned."

"How close did you get?" Jonathan asks around a mouthful of salmon, buttery garlic dripping down his chin. Kim catches it with a napkin. The mommy response is strong from daily use.

"Well, technically, it was still within the tree line, so maybe forty feet?" What I saw was mainly a massive, lumbering silhouette. I saw it, though, and that's what counts.

"So it could have just as easily been a raccoon and not a bear."

Chapter 7

He always was a bit of a dick. I keep it to myself. Kim has been my friend too long to let him rankle me.

"No," I argue, knowing it won't make a difference. "It wasn't a raccoon. At any rate, I hear they can be more aggressive than black bears."

"They have rabies," Jonathan tells us matter-of-factly.

"Not all of them. Raccoons are reputed to be wild enough without the deadly virus."

"From what I hear, you were pretty wild without rabies too." Kim nudges him sharply in the side, throwing him a nasty look.

See? Dick.

"It was college." Jonathan is not going to ruin my meal. The paella is to die for. "I needed the money," I joke. "Also, let us not forget your lovely wife was with me on all our excursions." I won't throw her under the bus. He can keep his version of the ideal woman he has of his wife. No doubt, today she is terrific, but she was a party girl of the first order back then. She put me to shame time and again.

Kim, her face crimson, says meekly, "It was a long time ago."

"Gone and forgotten, right, honey?"

She gives her hubby a nod. I want to kick him, but hey, that's me.

Adam hasn't said a word since the spa. He's just soaking in the space, which is truly lovely. A three-string quartet plays classical music in the corner, the waitstaff wears tuxedos, and nothing on the menu is within my price point. Not to say I don't have the money. I just believe no side dish is worth fifty dollars. Call me crazy.

Out of the blue, Kim says, "Tell us about cuddle bunny."

A sigh escapes my lips. "Oh, boy." I should have known she'd ask with her obsession over mysterious strangers. I've only shared the minimum, and it's killing her.

"He's my snuggle bunny," I rib her. "Get it right."

"Fine. Start with him. His stats. Story. How great he is in bed."

I choke on a shrimp, which forces Adam into action. He pounds my back, hands me my water, and begins to call out for a doctor. "I'm fine," I manage to croak before he causes a real scene or snaps my spine like a twig. The palm slamming into me feels like a baseball bat. I gulp down the water and take deep breaths to soothe the spasms.

Once everyone begins eating again, Adam asks, "So, who is he?"

I preferred him silent. Wishing I could avoid the question, I remind myself I'm among friends. It's okay to share a little.

Before I can begin, Kim cuts in. "He's the guy she's sleeping with."

"What?" Adam yells out louder than the atmosphere allows. Apparently, he wasn't paying attention the first time she ineptly described my relationship with Edge.

The people around us stop what they're doing, including the waitstaff. A microsecond of complete silence occurs before utensils begin rattling and people start moving again.

Jonathan says, "We're going to get kicked out if we don't stop behaving like it's an Applebee's."

We all burst out laughing, once more gaining the attention of those around us but also giving us the space to reset.

"Maybe we should just focus on eating," I suggest. "I think it's enough for now." The waiter is giving us the hairy eyeball. Telling my friend's story isn't coffee talk, anyway. I am glad when the moment passes, allowing dinner to continue without another hitch.

8

JORDAN

Back to silence, Adam tosses his keys on the kitchen island and begins shutting the lights off from the primary control in the hallway.

Taking my cue from him, I turn to head upstairs to bed, then decide against it. If he doesn't want me here, I can go somewhere else. Hell, I can probably camp in Kim's backyard. I'm used to locating water sources, so broken plumbing means nothing to me.

"Why aren't you talking to me anymore? Did I say or do something to offend you?"

We're standing in the foyer. The only light streams through the floor-to-ceiling sliders off the patio to the pool. Solar lights bounce lazily on the surface, and the reflection dances across our faces. Adam looks stern, almost menacing, and I brace myself for his response.

I see the muscles in his jaw clench before he says, "No. It's nothing." He won't look at me. That's new too.

"I can tell something has changed. Maybe I've overstayed my welcome." I'm punting here. It has only been a smidge over twenty-four hours. I thought I had at least enough charm for twice that amount of time. "It's okay, Adam. You didn't sign up for this, so I'll just pack and go."

"No," he responds quickly, leaving me optimistic that it's the truth. "Definitely not the case. You can stay as long as you like." Whatever was bothering him releases its hold, and he visibly relaxes. "Can I be honest?"

"Always. Always be honest with me, no matter what."

"It's snuggle bunny." Adam smiles as he says the silly name. "This is the dumbest thing, but when Kim indicated you were sleeping with him, it kind of threw me for a loop."

Adam's eyes dart to mine, and he holds the gaze and moves closer. He doesn't stop until we're standing toe to toe, bringing us almost level in my heels. "I got jealous. I barely even know you, but I felt possessive. You can sleep with anyone you like. I'm glad you have someone close to you out there."

I'm feeling warm all of a sudden. I hadn't noticed how kind Adam's brown eyes are or how clean his skin smells. Left momentarily believing I want to sleep with *him,* I close the gap and kiss him. He kisses me back, deeply. Desire twists powerfully in my belly.

He pulls back the slightest bit, and I feel the loss.

"What are you doing?" he asks before kissing me again, softly this time. Soft enough to weaken my knees.

"Kissing you."

"What about snuggle bunny?"

"He prefers to be called Edge."

"I don't care. Why did you kiss me?" He's still holding onto my hips as though preventing me from fleeing. I'm not going anywhere. Those kisses were sumptuous.

"I wanted to. And I want to again."

Taking a deep breath, he lets me go, running his fingers through his thick hair. Now I find myself wishing I could do that, as well.

Instead, I hear, "That sounds like a bad idea. Goodnight, Jordan. I'll see you in the morning."

He leaves me standing alone.

Chapter 8

Adam

I log onto Jordan's blog, looking for any information on this snuggle bunny/Edge guy, and find nothing. She has plenty of stories about run-ins with wildlife, rainy nights strong enough to infiltrate her tent scams, and different trail challenges she's met and overcome. I see pictures of her with various people and a dog here and there, but nobody stands out as particularly edgy or snuggly. Although one shot strikes me as having potential. Standing in front of a craggy mountain, Jordan balances on a rock with one foot, the other leg kicked high in a sort of standing split, while a huge man supports the raised foot with one finger. She's smiling while his look is lethal. Something about him looks familiar. Possibly his resemblance to a grizzly? Unable to put my finger on it, I keep searching.

I scroll down and read comments, focusing on their usernames, yet continue to find nothing. *I need to know who the hell this guy is!* I'm desperate to kiss her again. When she pressed her lips against mine, my mind went blank. All I could do was feel. Her soft lips and hot tongue played while the tips of her breasts grazed the front of my dinner jacket. The second kiss was even better. I was about to sweep her upstairs when my brain decided to work again. I don't sleep with women in relationships, period. And I don't indulge in pleasure of any kind. I thought it was so ingrained by now that I was impervious to feeling and wanting. One day and already, she has me tied in knots. *Ridiculous.* I need to get my head on straight and fast.

Knowing I'm not going to sleep anytime soon, I change into my swim trunks and head down for a few laps. Maybe it will douse the flame Jordan lit.

And maybe not. Jordan is there at the poolside, relaxing in one of the lounge chairs, a glass of wine in hand. Her body is angled to the side, the long dress accentuating the smooth flare of her hip. She looks stunning tonight. I compliment myself on my high level of restraint as I open the sliders and head out.

She sits up suddenly as though caught in the act of something illicit. "Sorry," she says. "Do you want me to go?"

"No. I told you, I want you to stay."

"No, I mean to bed or something..." Her voice trails off. Maybe this time, she picked up on the double entendre in the things she says. "Snuggle bunny is just that."

I pull another lounger close to hers and drop into it. "Just what?" I wasn't going to bring it up until morning, but this works.

"He's a friend I met on the trail. Technically, he goes by Edge, unless we're alone. It took a long time to get him to trust me, but once he did, we got close.

"I'll spare you the details, but he's had an awful time of life. He was in an industrial accident that changed everything in the blink of an eye. It left him, well, mutilated. That's the only word that could describe the level of injury. Because of it, his wife, Vicki, left him. And I mean the day after the accident. She just packed up and was gone by noon. She didn't even try to put her feelings aside to help out a person she professed to love.

"They never had children together, but he had two stepchildren. Sadly, Vicki took the kids, leaving no hope for visitation. For Edge to lose so much so quickly made getting close to another human herculean. But I'm awfully charming, as you've come to realize."

I like how her dimples show when she's trying to be funny.

"He learned to trust me. Since then, we cuddle to help us fall asleep. Not every night. He values his independence even more than I do, so he sometimes goes off for days at a time alone. We always meet back up, and when we do, we literally sleep together. I'm not the kind of gal that sleeps around. I wouldn't have kissed you if I was involved with someone else. I apologize if I gave you that impression."

We sit silently for a short time. I'm trying to come up with the right words to respond when Jordan has a realization.

"Hey. Are you dating someone else? Is that why you shut me down?" Her hand partially covering her mouth, she looks horrified at the thought.

"No, nothing like that. I haven't even *literally* slept with anyone in quite some time."

She smiles in relief and at my jest.

Chapter 8

"What kind of work did your friend do?"

"Robotics. He started when he was in the military. After his honorable discharge, he went to work for a private company. That's where the accident happened. Their focus is medical, not defense. Kind of ironic."

"He's lucky to have found a friend like you." I keep the conversation banal even if my insides are twisting. It all comes together. The picture on Jordan's blog, that day from hell, the life I once knew, gone forever.

She slides closer and lays her head on my shoulder, lost in her story. The contact feels good and helps reduce my anxiety level.

"I care a lot about him." I feel her smile spread across her pretty face. "He's as gruff as they come and about the size of Paul Bunyan, but he is my snuggle bunny."

"I'm glad you have someone to look out for you."

She pushes up to look me in the eyes. "Yeah?"

"Yeah." She lies back down against me. It's much better than to have to gaze into those trusting eyes of hers. "I was thinking earlier about how dangerous it is out there for women. I'm going to worry about you when you go."

"You're sweet but have no fear. I'm made of pretty tough stuff." Her voice fades as the long day and wine make her eyes droop. She cuddles in deeper to my side and quickly falls asleep. Planning to close my eyes for a second to savor the moment before carrying her up to bed where she'll be more comfortable, I follow her into slumber.

9

JORDAN

"Good morning," Adam greets me in a thick, still sleepy way. "What time is it?"

I hand him a mug of steaming coffee. "It's time to get up. I tried to wake you to watch the sunrise. It was spectacular."

He sits up, rubbing his face, relishing in those first sips of hot energy. It's nice to meet someone with a shared love of the bean.

"I'm a pretty heavy sleeper. Man, I've got a crick in my neck. I don't think this lounger has the same support as my bed."

"No. But I slept like a log too. Must have been the company."

He gives me a brilliant smile, one I would have regretted not seeing, like the sunrise. "You're very good at snuggling. You make it easy."

"Practice." It would be too easy to slide back into his embrace. I don't know why things changed between us. Our energy was light and fun at first. Now it crackles with fiery heat, even in the cool morning air. "How about that swim you came down for?" A dip in cold water should bring the temperature down a notch or two.

He puts his mug down on the concrete surround. "Race ya!"

He's in the water before I can tell him I haven't changed into my suit. Oh, well. What's the difference? I shimmy out of my dress and dive into the deep end. The water temperature is warmer than the ambient air. So much for cooling me down and keeping my thoughts off my handsome host. It feels exquisite against my skin, and I begin to swim laps.

Soon he is beside me, keeping pace, stroke for stroke. Our clip is languid and smooth, perfect for waking up the muscles and working out the kinks.

Finally, out of breath, I crawl halfway up the broad steps and sit beside him. "That was lovely. Is this salt water?"

"Nice, isn't it?"

"Luxurious."

He takes my hand in his, studying my raisin fingers. "I like having you here," he tells me.

"I like being here. It will be harder than normal to get used to the trail again."

"Because of the amenities?"

"Because of you."

He slips the tip of my index finger into his mouth, and my breath catches. He continues one at a time before kissing the center of my palm. I want his mouth on mine and scooch up a step to come up to his height. He cups my face and ravages my mouth. Pulling me to straddle his lap, my hands sink into his thick hair as he works on the clasp of my bra. Breasts free, he moves his lips ever so slowly downward until he pulls one hardened nipple into his mouth. Ecstasy is mine as I strain against him, wanting more, so much more.

The sliding door opens, and with it comes the icy chill I initially wanted. A slim, ash blond-haired woman stands gawking, seemingly nailed to the spot.

Clearing his throat, Adam says, "Good morning, Lisa. We'll be in momentarily." He pulls me closer, angling to cover my state of undress.

The housekeeper. Of course. I missed meeting her yesterday, being at the spa for so long. I didn't realize she came every day.

Hidden as best as I can be in the bright sunshine, I say, "Nice to meet you."

Lisa flies into motion, responding in kind, as she gathers our coffee mugs. She all but runs back into the house, and I feel awful.

Still seated on Adam's lap, I ask him, "What do I do now? Your housekeeper thinks I'm a slut."

He laughs out loud. "She does not! We're two adults enjoying each other's company. She should be the one to feel bad. Look what she ruined."

"It was fun." Adam holds up the straps of my bra, helping me dress; such a gentleman. As I slip my arms through, he kisses each peak before adjusting them properly and clasping them in. I clench again with want. *This stinks.*

"We have all day, Jordan. Let's make the most of it."

"But I want you," I say with a mix of desire and petulance in my voice.

He groans. "Don't talk that way when you're sitting on my lap. You're starting to torture me, woman."

"You want me to go?" I tease.

He blurts out, "I want you to come," frustration in every word.

At least I'm not alone.

He brings us both to stand. "Let's go inside. I'll make you breakfast."

"And more coffee." I shift priorities pretty quickly.

"Yes, my fiend. As much as you want." He kisses the tip of my nose and gets the door for me. I'd like to think, *I always have tomorrow*, but tomorrow is the day I leave.

※

Adam

I did it again. I get near Jordan, and I lose it. I told her last night we were a bad idea. We still are, especially knowing what I know now. But she has this magnetic pull and isn't leaving until morning. I can't just make out with her in my pool, and then hide. So, while Jordan is in her

Chapter 9

room, getting ready for the day, I call the only person who has enough information to help me navigate this new twist.

"Dude." Jonathan draws out the idiotic word way longer than necessary, and I regret the call already. He knows I can't stand it. We've been friends for decades, and I know annoyance comes with the territory, but I had held out the hope procreating would mature him. It hasn't yet. Like Jordan alluded to last night over dinner about her college experiences with Kim, Jonathan and I had our share of good times. I think we still do, but certain things still rankle me. This regressive form of speaking is a big one. "What's up?"

"A lot. I found out who snuggle bunny is."

"Who?" I can tell he's barely awake. I'm sure he stayed in his "man cave"—another personal irritation—long after Kim and he got home. Heavy drinking is another vestige of days gone by that he hasn't changed.

"The guy Jordan hikes with from time to time. Kim asked about him at dinner."

"Oh, yeah. Shit, whatever. It's just Jordan, you know."

"What does that mean?"

"You must have picked up on it. She's a floozy. All that mumbo-jumbo about living in the present moment, embracing what's right in front of you. She likes the hippy-dippy lifestyle, sex included."

"Why do you say that?"

"I wasn't kidding last night. Some of the stories I could tell you about her past."

"Enough." I cut him off. "Everyone has a history. I want to talk about now." He's being ridiculous. College was a long time ago, and everyone has a right to live life on their own terms.

"Look out, buddy. She's getting to you." He hears my frustrated sigh. "All right. Tell me who the guy is. I'm dying to know." He uses his underwhelmed voice.

"Neil Boudreau."

"Who?"

"How the hell much did you have to drink last night?" I raise my voice. "Neil Boudreau. The court case. The bodily harm. Any of this ringing a bell?"

"Oh, shit. Yeah. Okay. Hold on. I'm pouring my coffee now." The baby cries in the background. "Let me just get to the office." Thirty seconds later, he continues. "Okay, here's the deal. Jordan leaves tomorrow, so just stay away. She'll dance through a batch of daisies or something when she knows she's not going to get any attention. You were nice enough to let her stay with you. You don't owe her anything. Once you drop her off, you'll never have to see her again, and nobody will be any the wiser. This is not a big deal."

A heavy silence ensues. What Jonathan says makes sense. What I feel doesn't. I've always been a sensible guy. I smirk, realizing how quickly she's been changing that.

"Dude? You still there?"

"I'm still here. What if I want to see Jordan again?"

"Ugh! Seriously? She has gotten to you. Look, I admit, she's a nice-looking lady, but plenty of others are out there. Go get one of them."

"Like Payton?" Yet another reason I haven't dated in years. She also happens to be Jonathan's cousin.

"You got me. Set-ups don't always go as well as people hope."

"She tried to set my house on fire!"

"That was a misunderstanding. Payton didn't know how to turn off the grill." His voice lowers. "She hasn't been bothering you, has she?"

"No. I suspect I have the restraining order to thank for that." I never believed her story, but I also never actually saw her eat. The woman redefined lithe into something incredibly unhealthy.

"Overkill, buddy, but whatever makes you feel safe. Anyway, Jordan wasn't a set-up. You're supposed to be her host, nothing more. Keep it that way, and this will pass. Allow your baser instincts to be in control, and it's your funeral."

"Gee, you've been such a big help." I shouldn't be surprised. Jonathan takes nothing seriously, nothing to heart. I'm always shocked he's kept his marriage together as long as he has.

Not picking up on my blatant sarcasm, he says, "Hey. You're

welcome. You know you can call me with stuff like this anytime. I've got your back."

"Yeah. I'll talk to you later." I hang up without a clue for how to fill the next twenty-four hours.

Then the solution hits me. Daisies, hippies, floozies, oh my! Not that I believe Jonathan's take on Jordan at all, but the fair is in town. Complete with a church-run picnic, all sorts of old-fashioned outdoor games, and carnival rides. I bet she'll love it.

JORDAN

I answer my trail-beaten phone on the first ring. The deluge of texts beforehand drove me crazy, but I didn't respond because I knew who they were from and what the scoundrel had on his mind. All I wanted to do was upload on my blog about my zero days so I could enjoy the last few hours of downtime, but oh no. My ex-husband, Brett, wants to talk about porcelain dishes.

Skipping the pleasantries, I warn him, "If you say china plates, I'm hanging up. How many times do I have to tell you? I. Don't. Have. Them. Go out and buy your mother a new set because if it isn't in the storage container, it isn't anywhere."

"You were always such a joy in the morning," he responds. "But remember, you were in charge of the stupid yard sale. You insisted on having it." I picture his index finger pointing in the air. Brett loved to shove it right in my face when he'd fly off the handle. "Get the set back somehow, someway, or I'm calling Robert." Robert was his lawyer throughout our divorce.

"Call him. I'm not going to buy your mother a damn thing. The only thing you ever did to facilitate the divorce was to come over and cherry-pick through everything you wanted. I gave you no arguments with the understanding that what was left was going. And it went."

"Oh, yeah? That was all I did? How about giving you the lion's share of our savings and retirement?"

"Give? No, Brett, you shouldn't have cheated," I say bluntly. The line goes silent. I seem to have blown the wind out of his sails.

But no, he was just thinking and retaliates with, "If you had been half the woman Stacy is, we wouldn't have divorced. Oh, wait. You're not a woman at all, are you? You can't even make a baby.

"By the way, Stacy is doing great, and we're planning to deliver with a midwife. It's been so easy for her, this pregnancy thing. We missed you at the baby shower."

The line goes dead. Brett didn't even give me a chance to retort. Typical.

I curl up in a fetal position on the plush beige carpet, willing the tears not to come as they flow freely down my cheeks.

10

JORDAN

"This is one of the quaintest little towns I've ever seen," I tell Adam, who doesn't seem to notice I sound stuffed up. I refuse to let Brett ruin my day. The sun is shining, people around us are smiling and laughing, and I'm with a new friend. I have nothing to be sad about right here, right now.

No neon signs or big warehouse stores are in sight, just mom and pop specialty markets with handwritten sandwich boards. The carnival has all the vendors spilling onto the sidewalks, selling their wares. Jewelry, clothing, make-up, you name it, they have it. Everyone is super friendly, even to us looky-loos.

You can see the Ferris wheel and hear the carnival music getting louder as we get closer to the church. The white building with its tall steeple and graveyard with ancient, leaning stones makes you feel like you've taken a step back in time.

"That's where the food is, right?"

Adam laughs. "You and your appetite. Lunch is at noon on the dot." He looks down at the new watch I gave him after breakfast.

You can crave the craziest things once hiker hunger takes hold of your body. My cousin takes care of all my mailings, and in my most recent box, she included candy watches, sugary rainbow circles surround a bold yellow dial. I've been munching away on them since I arrived and wanted to share.

When Adam slipped it on next to his regular watch, I'd hollered, "Holy crap! Is that a Rolex?" I hadn't seen many of them, but their reputation makes seeing one, knowing one.

"Yes. A graduation gift from my grandparents."

"Nice grandparents."

He'd just shrugged as he bit off one of the blue circles.

The candy watch is stuck at one o'clock for infinity, or at least until it's eaten. Sadly, the real one now shows it is only ten-thirty in the morning. This did not bode well.

Adam raises an eyebrow. "You're hungry already, aren't you?"

"So hungry, yes."

We already played at the arcade. I kicked his butt in a dance-off. Then he served me my own in a car race.

"I think I see a fried dough cart up ahead. Mmm. I can smell it too." Grabbing his hand, I make a run for it.

"Is there anything as satisfying as eating fried dough at a carnival?" I sprinkle a thick layer of powdered sugar on mine, then Adam's.

"I could probably come up with a few things," he tells me, watching as I lick a stray crumb from the edge of my lip.

Shaking away his naughty thoughts, Adam leads me to a park bench to eat and people-watch between a bakery and the farmers market. What can I say? Food finds me.

"See anything else you like?" He points to the tchotchke store and jewelers across the street.

"Naw. I don't have any space to carry it. Porcelain cats and plastic Eiffel Towers don't help much on the trail."

"Ah, yes. I forgot that you're a wood nymph. Your time here will be over before you know it." He looks sad, and I work to cheer him up.

"You know what, though? I'd love a souvenir for the trail." I grab my phone. "Here, come closer. Say, 'Picnic lunch.'" I take the shot. "Oh, it's a keeper. Look." We're both smiling with our eyes open. I say we're a cute couple, even if he keeps pushing me away.

Chapter 10

"Nice. Would you send it to me?" Adam asks, pulling his phone from his back pocket.

"Way ahead of you."

A chime sounds on his end, and his smile returns when he sees the photo.

"Are you going to finish that?" I watch as he wraps the uneaten half of his dough to toss in the trash, a sacrilege. At my look of horror, he hands it over. Smart man.

"Should we go and check the itinerary?"

Wiping the grease from my face, I say, "Itinerary? Isn't the plan simply to have fun?" He takes everything way too seriously. That's probably why he's so successful.

"We need a plan. With so many things to fit in, we should prioritize."

I tuck my arm through his and march him towards the church. "Let me handle this."

A sweet elderly woman wearing a name tag hands us a leaflet. "Thank you, Gladys. Can you tell us which game is your favorite?" She's about five feet tall and adorable.

"Well," she says in a whisper, "I heard Father Pierce is worried because we have lots more water balloons than eggs. So if you want to do the egg toss, you'd best get in line now. But for my money, nothing is more fun than soaking your sweetheart on a hot summer day." Gladys is speaking to me, but she only has eyes for Adam. "You look just like my husband. A sturdy, nice-looking fellow he was." She tears up sweetly and tells me, "Hold on to him, honey. The good ones are hard to come by."

I give her a big hug for her loss and her assumption. She's right about most of it anyway. "Gladys, you have great taste. The balloon toss it is. Thank you."

"Good luck to you, darlings," she says and heads off to hand out another pamphlet.

I point to the left. "Oh, look, the sack race is lining up."

"I thought we were doing the balloon toss?" He's having such a hard time going with the flow.

"We will, but it's not until after lunch because there's no running involved. Grab a sack."

We join a row of ten other couples, most younger than us and two the same age. Only one twosome is older. I nudge Adam as we wait for the word "go."

"There's our competition."

"How do you figure? They have to be sixty if they're a day."

"That's the generation that did this sort of thing. As you said, they were out running their asses off every summer day." I point my thumb to the left. "These bozos sat on their butts, playing video games. Now, make me proud. Tap into that little boy who had to go in early and miss all the fun." I tighten my hold on the bag. "We aren't going down without a fight."

The caller yells out, "On your marks. Get set. Go!" And we're off. Things are going great. I'm looking ahead while keeping an eye on the couple to the right. The finish line is in sight.

And we win! I can't believe it. Adam wore loafers, so I thought we were done for. I reach for him, and he hugs me tight. I find myself missing him already.

"Good job, Jordan." He's grinning madly, proud of his part in the win.

"You too."

The game caller thrusts a googly-eyed bear in between us, our prize for winning, but we hardly notice.

Adam is pulling me closer, kissing me senseless.

"Wow. You really like sack races," I quip when Adam releases me.

"I really like you," he admits.

Adam

I tried to hold onto the day, but it slipped away all the same. Jordan and I played all afternoon like children. She is the most pleasant, down-to-earth lady I've ever met. She gave our sack race prize to a little girl we

Chapter 10

found crying after dropping her ice cream cone. She handed over a twenty-dollar bill when a teenage boy, desperately trying to win over a girl by knocking down glass bottles with a baseball, failed after ten attempts. He ran out of money before running out of hope. Jordan wished him luck and whispered something into the young girl's ear. She blushed and moved closer to her boyfriend. He went on to knock down the required amount, winning his pretty admirer a giant pink unicorn.

Now on top of the Ferris wheel, it blessedly stops to let more people board. I could stay like this forever. I'm pretty sure Jordan has fallen asleep, her head on my chest. Her strawberry smell blends with the scent of cotton candy, which she finished gobs of this afternoon.

I don't care what Jonathan says or thinks. He doesn't know a thing about Jordan. I feel as though I've only begun to tap the well and can't wait to know her even better.

How? I still have no clue.

11

JORDAN

Crazy to think this is it, but tomorrow morning, I'll be back on the trail. I'm ready. My muscles feel antsy, and though I thought it would be impossible to feel full before Thanksgiving, I've managed to do it with Adam's incredible meals and carnival snacks.

"Hey," Adam says quietly from the doorway of the bedroom. "Can I get you anything? Make you something for dinner?"

Inwardly I smile. I left the door open, hoping to see him before falling asleep. "No, thanks. Believe it or not, I couldn't eat another bite." A second wind hit me after the nap on the Ferris wheel, which is why I am packing tonight instead of in the morning. I plug in my phone, resting it on my trail runners to not forget it. I risk running out of juice if I don't remember to charge the vital connection to civilization at every in-town stop. I only pack what is essential to my physical and mental well-being with my ultralight sensibilities, and a portable battery didn't make the cut. Funny how some days, the backpack can still feel filled with heavy metals.

"Mind if I come in?"

"Please." I gesture to the bed.

He steps into the room but doesn't sit. "Are you all set with everything?"

Chapter 11

"Oh yeah. I've got it down to a science. Are you sure you don't mind dropping this box off at the post office? It's just the one, all packed and paid for."

"I'll do it right after I drop you off."

"Thanks." I continue loading goods, leaving a pile around me of to-be-determined when and where they go items. Already in my pj's, I'm prepared for whenever sleep finds me.

"Are you okay, Adam? You seem restive."

He takes a deep breath before speaking. "Can I tell you something?"

"Of course. Like I said last night, just make sure it's honest."

"That's a big one for you, isn't it?"

"Isn't it for everyone?"

He shrugs. "I don't know. It's a crazy world out there. I sometimes wonder if anyone is ever sincere."

I feel sad for him. Serving in his role as big-wig (lord knows I zoned out on his actual title), people surround Adam, but he has a loneliness about him that breaks my heart. "You should have someone you trust in your life. It's important."

"I trust you," he tells me, penetrating my soul with his gaze. His struggle is evident, as if he doesn't believe his own words.

"You should. I'll always tell you the truth."

"Good," he says before turning silent, leaving me in suspense.

Giving him space to gather his thoughts, I continue rounding up the last of my things spread haphazardly around me on the beige carpet and shove them into my pack. I leave out the toiletries I'll need in the morning, along with my clothes and new shoes. Finally, I am packed and ready to go at a moment's notice.

"So. Care to share? I don't want to rush you, but time's a-wasting, my gracious host."

He takes a deep breath and says, "You know what? It's nothing."

"Sure sounded like something."

He ignores me and changes the subject, such a male strategy. "Would you like to watch a movie?"

"Now?"

"Well, yeah. Unless you're going to stay, then we can watch it some other time."

"You're cute, but you don't mean that." I'm only half kidding. I know entertaining me has been a struggle for him. "Honesty, remember?"

Adam crosses the room in three steps to cradle my face in his hands tenderly. His voice is rough as he insists, "It is the truth." He slants his mouth over mine and kisses me deeply. A small moan escapes my lips, and he takes full advantage by exploring with his tongue. I pull closer, grasping his shirt in my hands as he plunders my mouth deliciously.

As abruptly as it began, he pulls back. "I'm sorry." He shakes his head as if to clear it. "Something happens to me when I'm around you. That's what I wanted to say. Even though I hardly know you, I dread dropping you off tomorrow." He clasps his hands behind his head as he forces his breathing pattern back down to normal.

I wonder what has him so nervous.

"This may be a bad idea, Jordan, but can I see you again?"

"Tell me what you're afraid of first."

Pain darts through his eyes before he blinks, and they're back to neutral. "I'm not afraid of anything."

"That's a lie, Adam. Everyone is afraid of something. Plus, you keep saying this is a bad idea. Why?" I wait for his answer, worrying he might bolt instead.

But finally, he says, "Because happiness isn't something I want in my life."

I laugh without thinking. Adam can't be serious. Except his dark expression suggests he is. "What do you mean you don't want happiness? Everyone wants that. I'm pretty sure it's the number one goal of humans everywhere."

"Maybe for most. You don't know much about me, Jordan, but I'm not a very good person."

I try to interject, but he stops me. "Wait. I haven't killed anyone or purposefully ever harmed another being. It's a lot more complicated than that. I don't deserve to be happy, so I don't seek it out. But then

Chapter 11

you came, and now all I want is you, and you make me happy. So what do I do?"

The hurt is back in his eyes. Whatever he did must have been awful, and I feel my belly heave. Brett was terrible enough. I don't need another dysfunctional man in my life to destroy my self-esteem and screw everything up. I've learned enough of those lessons to last a lifetime.

Still, I feel I know him more than he thinks. He is decent and kind. Look at what he's doing for Lisa. Not to mention opening his home to me at a moment's notice. He has a sister he's close to as well. No. Adam is one of the good guys.

I go to him and wrap my arms around him tight. It takes a moment, but soon he relaxes against me, and we remain cocooned in the quiet of the room until I break the silence. "I know who you are, Adam." My ear rests against his chest, enjoying the strong beat of his heart. "You don't have to tell me your story." I add, "Yet," and continue. "But you will someday, and we'll figure out your problem then. For now, let's go watch a movie. There will be popcorn, right? Otherwise, I'm out."

"I knew who I was inviting before I came up. Popcorn, candy, and soda. Unless you want wine."

"Beer."

"Beer it is." He kisses my forehead before taking my hand and leading me to the twelve-seat theater two flights down.

❧

Adam wakes me long after the movie ends, as the sun rises, trailing tiny kisses down the length of my neck. Every nerve ending fires up beneath the tender touch. Apparently, the best part of waking up is not Folgers in your cup.

We readjust so he's pressed against my back on our adjoining armless theater seats. He envelopes me in a spoon position. "Don't leave," he whispers.

I angle my head for a kiss. "I have to go."

"Fine." He sounds cross, but I know he's kidding. "But come back. Promise you'll come back to me."

My heart melts. "I bet you say that to all your unexpected guests."

"Only the ones who stink to high heaven and eat me out of house and home."

Before offense can take hold, I realize I don't have a leg to stand on.

Adam kisses my frown away, and all is forgiven. I push back to look him in the eyes. "My offer still stands. You can go camping with me anytime. Let me know when, and I'll let you know where."

He laughs. "As I said, I'm not much for the outdoors. How about I get us a hotel room for one of your zeros?"

I'm rubbing off on him. He just used trail-speak.

"I suppose that would work. How about Massachusetts? I'll give you a week's notice to set something up."

"Done. You could give me an hour's notice, and I'd be there."

"I think it's at least a six-hour drive from here."

"Okay. I'll keep a suitcase packed." He kisses me again. "Or you could save me the hassle and stay."

"All right, that's it. I better go before you get all kidnappy." I jump up to head to the bathroom.

"That's not a word," he calls out as I go upstairs for my last shower for a while.

"Here we are," Adam announces the obvious in a forlorn voice. "Why do I feel like I'm losing something I'll never get back? How can parting feel devastating after only three days?"

"Because I'm awesome." I joke though I agree with his sentiment. I want to stay, but I need to go. Knowing it will only get harder the longer I wait, I ask him to open the back door, so I can grab my stuff.

"I'll call you every night." Adam talks foolishly while holding my pack, allowing me to easily slip my arms through the straps.

Chapter 11

He's been making absurd comments like this the entire drive. It's been a long time since I felt both seen and desired by a man. It's nice.

He told me he would hire me a Sherpa. "Strength in numbers" was his reasoning. He had also pointed out my fresh manicure. "You don't want to break a nail, do you?" I gave him an anti-sexism smack for that comment.

Then he said he would drive me the length of the trail, and we could sleep in bed and breakfasts along the way. "I read that no official board checks this sort of thing. Technically, you will have traveled the entire trail, so, yeah, let's do that." He held out his phone. "Here. Google the next hotel and make a reservation."

I just shook my head. "No. It is required you walk it to have bragging rights. So, stop being a nudge. This is a personal goal, and I'm doing it with or without your consent, Mr. I-Was-A-Complete-Stranger-To-You-Three-Days-Ago."

Now, as he joins me at the back of the SUV, I say in a firm, no-nonsense voice, "No more discussion, okay? I have to do this."

"Fine. We'll do it your way." He grasps both my hands and looks into my eyes. "All joking aside, I do know how important this is to you. I support you one hundred percent. I just need you to know how much I've grown to care about you. You're such a unique and wonderful woman."

"Thank you. I had a great time. I'll miss you." I rub my hand against his recently shaved cheek, pulling him close for a kiss. I hug him tightly before stepping back. "But I have to go."

He hands me the trekking poles.

"Massachusetts?"

"Yes," I tell him. "I'm already looking forward to it."

"Me too."

I wave as I cross the macadam to the trail. "See you later."

"You will." He doesn't sound convinced.

Once I'm alone under the thick canopy of trees, the ground solid beneath me with the unique and distinct scent of the Appalachian Trail wafting up my nose, I feel I've come home. I'm surprised at how natural the pack on my back feels and how quickly I find my usual pace. I was afraid civilization would spoil me for good, especially after meeting Adam.

I had envisioned the visit would be lonely and awkward, staying with a stranger. But it was the exact opposite. I felt an immediate connection with him. We had so much fun together, and his kisses were enough to convince me his lovemaking would be extraordinary.

It would have been too easy to stay with Adam and enjoy his luxurious lifestyle, but I would have missed this. And worse still, I would have lost myself. I won't let that happen again.

I reach an expansive pasture and raise my face to the warm sun. Bumblebees lazily gather pollen on wildflowers as crickets strum a rhythm. As I often do on this adventure, I wax poetic. And who but Robert Frost would come to mind at a time like this? So I recite "The Road Not Taken" aloud. "'Two roads diverged in a yellow wood… I took the one less traveled by, And that has made all the difference.'"

12

JORDAN

"Come on, say it. You missed me." I'm gleeful. My snuggle bunny waited for me. He blames it on twisting his ankle, but that's just his machismo talking.

"I can take you or leave you." Edge slings one arm across my shoulders. I know the physical touch shows how much he cares, but what he says is also true. It's how we became so close so fast. We have no expectations, no promises, just a simple and easy presence between us. I love his quiet, reserved personality. I tell him he loves me for my open heart and accepting nature. I think he believes me. However, most people we meet don't get it. They are supposed to use our trail names, but they tend to use "Mutt and Jeff" or "Felix and Oscar" instead.

"You shaved." I rub his face in my hands. "I'm going to like this much better when we go to sleep."

"Yeah. It's too frickin' hot. It was driving me crazy. Plus Wendy—" He stops mid-sentence.

Glee has ratcheted up to ecstatic. "What did you say? Who is Wendy?"

"No one." He blushes. My Edge blushes. Never in a million years would I have believed it.

"She's somebody, snuggle bunny. And you're going to tell me." I know his Achilles heel, so I begin to sing.

"Ugh! Stop!" He's covering his ears and trying to run at the same time. "Not the pop tart. That sorry excuse for music has single-handedly ruined parties for me forever."

"You ready to talk, or should I continue?" The song Edge hates most is my go-to whenever I think a bear might be around or when I night hike. The ditty keeps things away from you, trust me. I open my mouth to belt out the rest, and he finally relents.

"All right, but you don't need to know everything."

"I disagree, but share what you like."

"We met during my second thru-hike. Wendy worked at one of the resupply stores in Tennessee. We ran into each other again this year and started texting every day."

"Hey, I should have known about that." I'm hurt. Friends share this sort of stuff.

"I said you don't need to know everything."

I stick my tongue out at him.

"When I rolled my ankle, she was visiting with her sister, who was having a cast taken off her arm. We ended up sitting in the same orthopedic office in a weird coincidence, waiting for our appointments. We met for lunch, laughed a lot. And now I'm here walking with you."

"Bullshit!" I burst out.

"Every word is true."

"No. I accept the validity of the content. I'm calling bullshit on the banality of the details. Nobody blushes about laughing over lunch."

"I like her, okay? Can't you just drop it?" He storms off.

Oops. It looks as if I crossed a line. I follow Edge, giving him the space he needs to settle down. He's never held a grudge with me, and I don't expect it to happen now. But when lunchtime comes and goes, he doesn't stop. He just grabs a handful of nuts and keeps up a punishing pace. Wendy must be something else to cause this much of a reaction.

When the sun begins to descend, and we still haven't had dinner, I call out, "Enough. If you're going to be a shit for much longer, keep on walking, bunny. I'm setting up camp right here." I am beyond hungry.

Chapter 12

Granola and dried fruit only get you so far on a twenty-three-mile day. I crave comfort food, something fierce. A carbohydrate-laden meal to release endorphins and settle me down for a good night's sleep.

High heat and humidity have me sweaty, cranky, and itchy. I'm looking forward to having a thorough sponge bath directly after feasting.

Too hungry to set up my tent, I start rummaging through my pack for my stove and propane. Only I can't find the propane. I check every pocket, nook, and cranny. Nothing. I'll have to start a fire if I want a hot meal. And tonight, I *need* a hot meal, so I change tactics. Keeping out only what I'll use for dinner and sleep, I find a distant tree with a stable branch to sling up my pack. On my way back, I gather enough small twigs, sticks, and dry leaves to start a fiery blaze.

Having noticed my lack of a heat source, Edge has already made a circle with a pile of round rocks. In silence, we work together to get a flame going and begin boiling the water.

Tonight is a special freeze-dried meal: biscuits and gravy. I'll be as full as a tick if I finish both servings, but I'm hungry enough to meet the challenge.

Edge appears to be softening as he pours water into both our pouches before folding down the tops. We wait the longest ten minutes known to man.

"Where do you think you lost your gas?"

"You better hope I lost my gas. Bedtime comes pretty early around these parts." I make him laugh, so I know he let go of the grudge.

"Look, I'm not ready for details. When I am, you'll be the first to know. All right?"

"Okay. I'm sorry I was intrusive. It's not our thing."

"It's okay. By the way, Miss Inquisitive, you haven't told me about your week of zeros."

"It wasn't for that long." I punish him for calling me out on my slacker break by scooping up some of his pasta. It's surprisingly creamy and delicious.

"It was wonderful." I fill him in on all the G-rated details, now understanding why he held back in his retelling of Wendy and their romance. No way was I going to mention being caught by the housekeeper. Edge would have it for breakfast, lunch, and dinner.

"I can't picture you in a dress."

"Why not? I'm a feminine kind of gal."

He gives me a look that disagrees.

"I'll prove it." I scroll through the pictures on my phone and locate a few from my visit with Adam.

The night we dressed for dinner, Jonathan waited for the valet at the restaurant. Adam and Kim followed me into a spacious gazebo around the back, still decorated from a wedding earlier in the day. Satin ribbon bunting entwined with bouquets of blue hydrangea and white roses hung all around us. I stuck my face in every bloom. Kim had wanted to get a picture, so we handed our phones to Adam.

I pass mine over to Edge now. "Here. Proof."

After settling his food on a safe, flat spot, he takes it. "Fuck!" he bursts out, throwing the phone, which comes to land within inches of the fire.

What the hell? Me in a sexy dress can't be that much of a shocker. Edge is hyperventilating as he paces, trying to tug nervously on a beard that is no longer there.

"What is it?" I ask, my eyes wide.

Incapable of speech, he raises his hand toward me in a fist, index finger pointed in my face. I rear back as memories of heartache and abuse flood my mind. Before I can gather my wits, he grabs his pack and flees into the night, phantasmic in his element.

I am at a complete loss as to why Edge freaked out. It certainly wasn't the dress. Or Kim. Nothing that lives in the woods scares him. I could see no evidence of an attack. Aliens hadn't hovered above us in a glowing spaceship, threatening an anal probing. I sit by the fire, scarfing up both our meals, going over every potential possibility.

Forget about my heart jumping into my throat when he raised his hand the same way Brett used to. I know Edge wouldn't ever strike me,

Chapter 12

but, for all the world, it felt like I was back in my master bedroom with Brett reading me the riot act about how I was damaged goods. I could use a snuggle bunny right about now to help me settle, but he's hopped off. Who knows if it's for good?

With my adrenals revved up, I'm never going to fall asleep. I turn on my headlamp and dismantle camp for a night hike, making sure the fire is out. Walking always clears my head and gives me the insight I need to solve problems. As I start to pocket my phone, I accidentally hit the on button. There, as bright as day, is the last image Edge had seen before leaving. It wasn't the shot in the gazebo that set him off. Curiously, it was the next one—me smiling next to Adam at the fair.

13

ADAM

*J*ordan is gone, and I'm back at work with fourteen other men and women surrounding the board room table. As usual, Jonathan sits to my left while the law team's head attorney is to my right.

We've been testing a new type of software in our robotics lab to help fine-tune brain surgery mechanics, particularly in children. The micro-level of size, coupled with the macro need for next-level precision, has proven challenging. As CEO and majority shareholder, the buck stops with me.

Thoughts of my princess of the pun get in the way of what Kashmir is saying. Luckily, most of it is the same rigamarole the last two bidding companies have given us. He'll have to say something beyond the generic to get my go-ahead, having bid three times what the competition did. Knowing I'll revisit Jordan and our interludes throughout the day, I refocus my attention.

"While my team at Dynamic Design primarily focuses on robotics use with the military," says Kashmir as he glances around at the many faces turned in his direction, "our factories can handle any protocol. We have the machines to create the prototype you are looking for and

Chapter 13

the robots to help us fine-tune it to the microscopic level you need while retaining the information you want. Plus, we have the safety factor. Our company is top in its field. We work slowly, yes, but methodically. In twenty years, we've had zero violations. If, at any phase, safety even hints at being an issue, we slow down and regroup. Stop entirely if necessary.

"We seek progress and unquestionably money." Smirks abound. Everyone knows why they are here. "But not at all cost. Only for the advancement of therapeutic care. It would be madness to risk lives under the excuse it could one day save a life."

We have all read the prospectus, and Kashmir was nothing if not thorough. No one has any follow-up questions after he finishes his speech. Shutting down his computer and storing it in his messenger bag, he tells us, "That's all I have. I appreciate your time. If you have any questions later, please forward them to my email. Thank you. I'll look forward to hearing back from you regarding your decision."

In this post-handshake world, he leaves without fanfare.

I send a text to my assistant, two seats down, to start making inquiries. The man seemed authentic, but I want to see the data on safety. I'm certain Dynamic Design was aware of the catastrophe here at Advanced Automation. The entire industry chimed in when we had to close the factory and be inspected by every known local and federal government agency. We were all relieved when we finally got the go ahead to start up again. I have to be sure whether Kashmir's stats are spot on or if he's blowing smoke, saying the right thing to stand out.

"We'll cast votes by the end of the day on Friday, and I'll make the final decision on Monday." I'm already ninety percent there. "Thanks, team." I leave with Sheila, while everyone else stays for the catered lunch.

※

Looking out my tenth-story window into the side of another concrete building, I'm wondering where Jordan is now. We haven't spoken, so I don't know how far she's traveled or if she's run into her snuggle bunny. I feel a pang in my stomach at the thought of them exchanging stories.

Preferring to be alone with my thoughts, instead, my partner waltzes right into the office. Sheila left early to meet with the only ex-client of Dynamic Design, the one negative opinion she could find. Her leave-no-stone-unturned attitude has saved my ass numerous times, and I trust her detective work implicitly. Still, it leaves my door unguarded.

"Dude."

I cringe. "Jonathan, at least be professional at work."

"What crawled up your ass?" He sits casually, one leg thrown over the arm of the leather chair.

The annoyance is because he interrupted my daydreams, and Jordan has a much prettier face.

"Sorry. Just going over the options. Which company did you prefer?"

"Considering how close they were in their strategy, go with the cheapest. Which one?" He snaps his fingers to recall the name. "Phased Vision? And bonus, their rep had the best gams."

"For fuck's sake, you're married, and she wasn't a rep. She's the CEO. When are you going to step into the new millennium? Women are no different from men in—"

Jonathan cuts me right off. "They are totally different from men." His eyebrows rise and fall suggestively. "You know what I'm saying?"

"I'm not talking anatomy. In the workplace, women aren't any different than men. Have some respect, would you? You're supposed to be a role model, Number Two."

His eyebrows draw together in a dark scowl when I call him that, but he deserves it. He's been impossible lately. Not only is our relationship suffering, but working with him is now fraught with bitterness. It's not that I didn't know the adage of never working with friends or relatives going into this venture, but with whom else would you start a company? A stranger?

Chapter 13

We hit it off from the moment we met in grammar school. Jonathan was the class clown, and I was the bookworm. I helped him with his homework, except for math—his genius is narrow but profound. Priding myself in not kowtowing to his threats of bodily injury, I never completed any papers for him in other subjects. He helped me have a circle of friends. I have no doubt they tolerated me from grammar school through college because we came as a boxed set. None of them are around today.

The reason I thought we would be better than the statistics, mixing friendship and business, was because we had always worked together, and it went well. We profited in grades and cold hard cash from lemonade stands and choosing each other as science lab partners.

In the last few years, it's like we hit a fork in the road. One of us continues down the path of maturity, while the other has stayed put. You would think having a baby would have made him the grownup. Some days I wonder if Kim ever feels the same as I do: When she gave birth, she got a two-for-one deal, Jonathan regressing before her eyes.

"Yeah. I would have bought the extra five percent if I had known you'd turn into such an old man so fast. Lighten up, Adam. You only live once."

"We're forty. It's time to start acting your age. But beyond that, I'm afraid I have to disagree. I say we go with Dynamic Design. They have all the credentials, plus they were the only company to stress safety. That sealed the deal for me."

"I was afraid of that. Look, it's time to move on. We can save money and still get a great company. These are the top three firms specializing in robotics in the world. They didn't get to those heights without dotting their i's and crossing their t's." He casually scratches at the hem of his pants. It's one of his tells. He has something more to say. "Kim spoke with Jordan last night," he mentions almost righteously.

"Oh, yeah?" I admit I'm a bit jealous. I kind of thought I might be her first phone call back on the trail.

"I guess she and that teddy bear—"

"Snuggle bunny," I correct him.

"Who the fuck cares?" he growls. "They had a falling out. He stormed off during a campfire dinner one night, and she hasn't heard from him since."

"Any idea why?"

"Not specifically. Something about a picture. I don't pay too much attention when Kim tells me stuff about Jordan. What do you care?"

I'm silent long enough for him to fill in the blank.

"I warned you, bro. This is not going to end well if you don't stop all this pursuing Jordan nonsense. She got him to open up, you know. She's a persuasive lady; no question about that."

"Watch what you're saying. You're already on thin ice." It's bad enough the way he views women in general. I'm not going to sit here while he tears my woman apart with foolish stories from when she was barely through with childhood. College was a lifetime ago. Jonathan seems to be the only one who can't move on.

"Fine. But remember, this isn't the sort of thing you share with just anyone. Jordan got Neil to tell her his story after what, a week?" Incapable of not letting his tongue get away from him, he doesn't step over the line I just drew about Jordan but takes a hurdler's leap. "I bet she's fucking him."

Not a violent man by nature, I see red. My chair goes flying into the wall as I shove back to stand. "Get out of my office!" I yell, pointing at the door.

Jonathan scrambles to his feet, hands in a defensive posture. "Dude. Seriously, you need to calm down. This is Jordan we're discussing. No big deal."

Using all my willpower to keep me from jumping over the desk to throttle him, I threaten, "You have three seconds to get out, or you're a dead man."

"Don't say I didn't warn you." Jonathan slams the door on his way out.

I don't know what to make of any of this. I suspect the fallout is something personal between Jordan and Neil, and I hope they haven't

Chapter 13

figured out my connection in all this. Jonathan is a moron if he thinks his lies can change how I feel about Jordan. But, at least he's gone.

One thing I do know for sure: they are not having sex. Even Jonathan knows it's true. So why would he say that?

14

JORDAN

It's been three days on the trail since I've seen the sun. Wear the raincoat, don't wear the raincoat; it doesn't matter either way. Soaked slick as a seal, I have two choices: my sweat or the ambient mist. Picking the fog, I shove the jacket between my back and the pack if I change my mind. Or the weather decides to change. A deluge would feel heavenly right now. The promise of a poor man's shower and relief from the weighty humidity has me daydreaming.

"Dummy!" I call out as I slip, slamming into the rocky ground knees first. Pennsylvania might be known for its beautiful pastures, but this Appalachian Trail section is more a scramble than a walk.

Some days are better than others. The knowledge doesn't help when today happens to be one of the downer ones. I sit and remove my first aid kit and a bottle of water. After a long swig, I use a soaked bandana to wipe off the blood and clean the wounds. I'll get a ration of shit for this next time I run into one of the hikers I know, mainly because they're deep enough to need Band-aids, leaving me looking like a little kid and not the intrepid thru-hiker I envision myself to be. A twig or something has poked a deep hole in my forearm. So I give it an extra rinse, squeeze out all the blood I can, and wrap it with the bandana. That should do it.

Chapter 14

Eating a granola bar and a box of raisins, I torture myself with pictures of me in Adam's arms, in his pool, and sitting in his kitchen, eating an omelet. His cinnamon buns, not to mention his physical ones, have my primal desires cranked up high.

Now I've done it. It's too early for a scheduled meal, but I'm unable to have Adam, so I focus on food. Salivary glands in overdrive, I pull out my lunch provisions, make two trail pizzas, and gobble them down. I guess it'll be noodles for dinner. I set them up for a cold cook before I clean up and take the first step of the next section of my walk.

I'm alone on Bake Oven Knob, usually a popular spot for day hikers and section hikers. Well, almost alone. I hear chipmunks chirping around me as they scuttle through the underbrush. My mind wanders again, and I slow my pace so I can remain upright. I've got guys on the brain, and I'm struggling.

My marriage was fine. It wasn't a fairy tale, but Brett and I got along well enough. After the initial excitement of the wedding, honeymoon, and setting up a house, we got into the day-to-day routine typical of any married couple. Work, promotions, Saturday date nights, sunny tropical vacations, and unexpected home repairs. Nothing earth-shatteringly horrible, but nothing I'd define as great, either.

We weren't trying to have a baby, but we weren't not trying. After two years, it seemed it should have happened. We had all the standard tests. I assumed it was Brett because he was never particularly virile or lusty. Okay, maybe that's Jordan, the ex-wife talking, but for sure, he was no Adam.

But the infertility was me. Idiopathic, meaning the medical community has no idea why, so try as I might, it won't happen.

I was open to exploring options, but Brett was examining Stacy at this point, unbeknownst to me. I don't know why he didn't leave sooner. He blamed it all on infertility, saying the ugliest things about me he possibly could as though he had been saving them up for when they would pack the biggest punch.

I was all for a clean, no-fault divorce until I saw them canoodling on a park bench across the street from my job. He knew I went out for lemonade at noon every day to soak up the sun and see the sky, proving he's a bit of a psycho. I'm both horrified and relieved I didn't know it during our relationship. Stacy can have him. I got the bank account. It may not have been enough for champagne and caviar, but any amount was indeed a far better deal.

With all this baggage, I wonder about my visit with Adam. Should I even pursue it? Beautiful as it was, it was such a short time. If I didn't know Brett well enough in years, how could I possibly get a sense of the real Adam in days?

I'm on this trail to let go of all my conditioned beliefs and discover who I am and what I want, exclusive of anyone else. I promised to see Adam in Massachusetts. Maybe that will help me decide. I have hundreds of miles left to figure it out, so I focus on putting one foot in front of the other.

❧

I keep looking at my phone, but I still can't tell what time it is. Oh, I see the numbers, but they make no sense. What exactly is three o'clock? I pause to absorb the meaning of the question, searching my mind for the answer, only to come up with more confusion.

It's so hot. Every step is laborious; everything feels close. The leaves brush against me, causing itchiness to break out, crawling up my arm and down my torso. I can't seem to stop fussing with my bandages, so I rip them off as I go, leaving a trail of detritus behind me.

Wait! I remember I don't litter. A picture of a younger me flashes through my head. I'm going door to door down the dreary halls of our apartment building, trying to convince my neighbors of the importance of not littering, especially in the playground. They were nice enough, but no one joined the fight. The trash continued to pile up. Plastic bottles used for drugs, syringes, candy wrappers, and the such built up until a wayward wind blew the light stuff against the rusted metal fence. The heavier junk is probably there to this day, moldering in the tall grass.

Retracing my steps, I can't find any of the adhesive little fuckers.

Chapter 14

After spinning in circles, I get too dizzy to continue and plop down on my butt. What is wrong with me? Chalking it up to the rainforest-like heat and humidity, I spy something light brown on my shoe. *My Band-aid found me!* I pull it off with two others that tagged along, cradling them close to my heart. Tears fill my eyes when I think of how I almost lost them. I cry for what may be an inappropriately long time before placing them safely into my bag.

I check my phone. Three-ten. Is that a long time from three o'clock? I puzzle until the digital number hits three-twelve. Still meaningless, I get off my duff and continue forward.

Or do I?

I turned around so many times, I'm not sure if I'm heading in the right direction. Believing I may be backtracking, I sit down on a flat rock by a small brook that looks familiar. I'll just take a drink and figure this all out. What is the meaning of time? Where am I? And wondering: Am I going the right way? These questions take all the brain space I have available.

So I sit. I ponder. I sweat.

Then I start laughing. How is it that I never noticed how hilarious watching moving water could be? It dances and swirls; it gurgles too. My abdominal muscles are burning from the clenching, and I try to calm down. It works until a leaf floats by, and I'm off again, worse than ever. The tears flow, the abs ache, and I can no longer remain on my perch from the strength of the gales. On my side, I clutch my belly while choking on giggles that fight to be released, each vying to exit first. Space in my throat is limited, and the backup is sure to kill me. *What a great way to go!* I laugh harder still. *I know something!* A miracle.

The crack of a twig stops me mid-chuckle. Remaining on the ground, I push myself up to seated. I hear voices, male voices, along with the rhythm of their footfalls coming ever closer. Paranoia sweeps through me, and I try to stand. But my legs aren't working right. Weak and shaky, they won't hold my body weight with my pack still attached, and I fall back into the mud. Pain shoots through every muscle fiber, and bile floods my throat. Two burly men with full beards find me vomiting watery sputum into the puddle beneath my face.

"Jeez." The taller of the two lumberjacks elbows the other. "Take a look at her."

The men close in, inspecting me like a bug. I pray my condition will keep them away, smelling as I do. Too bad that it doesn't, so keeping quiet is the only strategy that arises to protect me.

"Look at those legs," says the one with the blue backpack.

I don't have the strength to gaze down at myself. *Why are they fixating on me?*

"Yeah, pretty sweet," agrees the other man leaning against his hiking poles.

Even my addled brain can recognize this was not the response I wanted. Finding anything sweet about me at this point meant they were sicker than I was. And I must be sick. I've never felt like this before.

I try to find the words to reason with them, but everything I say comes out like gibberish. My lips feel weird, but it's their faces that have me terrified. The flesh won't stay on their heads. No matter which one I focus on to plead my case, his face keeps slipping down toward his chest. Thick rolls of skin and hair collect at his neck.

One tells me, "Just stay still, babe," while the other wrestles the pack from my back. Life as I know it fades to black.

❧

When I come to, I'm lying on the side of the road. Tied and trussed like a pig on a spit, I struggle with the wrapping.

My captor calls out from far away, "Hey!"

I work faster, but the ties are too tight. I can't even roll over in the hopes of stopping a car. Not everyone is a psycho intent on harming me. The next passer-by might be my ride to freedom.

Too late. His feet are in my face, and his hands encase my shoulders, holding tight, forcing me to lie still. "Stop. You're going to hurt yourself."

Finding my voice, I croak, "You'd like that, wouldn't you? Let me

Chapter 14

go!" I try to spit on him, having no other weapons, but I'm too dehydrated to accrue any saliva.

He has the gall to laugh. "Just stay where you are. You'll be safer that way."

Safety first is my motto. I take his advice to heart and stop moving. I don't know how to get out of this, but it's not happening now. I have too many menacing men making sure I don't escape.

I hear one flag down a car. "Over here."

"Wow. You guys weren't lying," a female voice says.

I think she may be my ticket out and try to persuade her with my words. Alas, they have failed me again. All I manage to get out is, "What is time?"

"Five in the evening."

"No!" I yell. My throat feels as raw as hamburger meat. "What does it mean?"

Her laugh is genuine and kind, so why am I still constrained after being unceremoniously tossed into the backseat of her car?

"Oh, dear." She touches my burning forehead with fingertips like ice cubes. I cringe from the frost. "Trying to find deeper meaning in abstract concepts is not a good sign, especially in her condition."

I try to bite her, unsuccessfully.

She tells her coconspirators, "Let's go, guys. They're expecting us."

I have no backpack, no understanding of time, and no one knows where I am. Plus, the giggles are back. One of the droopy-faced men turns to look at me, and I go over the deep end to goofy-town.

15

JORDAN

Bright lights shine all around me. Still, I know I'm not dead because everything hurts, from the top of my head to the tips of my toes. A migraine-level headache crashes between my ears like high tide during hurricane season. I have no intention of opening my eyes until the daylight fades to dark.

Nausea changes my mind. I sit bolt upright, both hands covering my mouth to hold back the tsunami. Fluid, powered by reverse peristalsis, ejects through every available space, soaking the white blanket beneath me, soiling the oversized salmon pink gown I find myself in.

No longer hot as a skillet, I lie back wet, stinky, and shivering from the chills. The door to my left swings wide, and a woman in blue scrubs enters the room.

"Oh, honey. Let me help you clean up." The nurse is large and in charge and gets to work. Within seconds, I'm disrobed and re-gowned after a brisk rub down with a sudsy washcloth. She shoos me into a pleather chair and strips the bed, making it in record time.

I climb back in to find the bedding is warm and wrap myself up in the crisp fabric. Another woman comes in on squeaky rubber-soled shoes, less confidently but bearing food. I'm not particularly hungry.

Chapter 15

My nurse speaks for me. "She'll eat later, Anne. Give it to Mrs. Wallace."

Without missing a step, Anne walks past us and beyond the curtain to my right. I hadn't noticed I wasn't alone.

"Where am I?" I ask quietly.

"You are at St. Agatha's, my dear. You are going to be quite all right after you rest up a bit. Your doctor should be starting rounds shortly and can answer all your questions. Now, do you have any pain?"

"I have an awful headache."

"That's the dehydration," she tells me as she loads up a new bag of saline solution to drip into my arm. "This should help, but I'll get you some medicine too. Any allergies?"

"No."

"Great. Sit tight, and I'll be right back. I'm Maddy, by the way."

While I wait, I notice Mrs. Wallace has her TV on, and she's watching a popular morning show. *That can't be right.* Now that the heat is gone, I can understand time. I last checked my phone at twelve past three in the afternoon. (At least, I think I did.) How can a show that airs at nine in the morning be on? Maybe a repeat, I convince myself as Maddy returns with my pills.

She watches as I swallow them, and from the serious look on her face, I almost expect her to demand I lift my tongue to prove I took them.

"You're lucky you have friends, Jordan, dear. You were in quite a state when you arrived."

"Friends?" I try to think. What friends? I haven't seen Edge in weeks, and I don't have anyone else to rely on, at least not close by. "You mean my kidnappers?" It sounds stupid as it comes out, but that's who they are, plain and simple. I'm about to ask to speak to a cop when she tsks.

"Even worse than I thought. Those weren't kidnappers, honey. Those boys saved your life."

"No. They found me and took advantage. They were ogling my legs and tied me up, leaving my body on the side of the road until their ride came. Who knows what they did to me after that. Have they been arrested? Can I speak to the police while I'm here?"

Maddy adjusts my blanket, ignoring my questions. "You know what? Get some rest, and I'll see about having Dr. Matthews putting you first on his rounds."

Without waiting for a response, she leaves me once again. I am tired, so instead of pondering on my predicament, fat chance it will get me anywhere anyway, I roll over and fall asleep.

※

"Jordan? Can you hear me?"

"They can hear you on the next block," I murmur as I struggle to sit up.

A tall man stands by my bedside, his laptop on my overbed table as he writes notes.

"Oh, good. You're awake. I'm Dr. Matthews. Maddy thinks you're a tad confused about all that has transpired lately. I'll give you the run down, and then you can ask any questions after. Good enough?" He's tall and thin with glasses that tend to slip down his nose. Whenever he adjusts them, he also flips his banged cowlick back. It's a boyish move that, for some reason, makes me feel relaxed in his presence.

"Good enough." I'm interested in filling in the gaps.

Reading from the screen, he continues. "Two men, Pack Rat and Juilliard, brought you into the ER at eight last night. After a short struggle—" He looks over his glasses at me. "My notes say you were quite feisty and verbose, preferring profanity to reason."

I relent. "That might sound like me. Go on."

"The orderlies got you in a wheelchair, and the ER staff checked you in as delirious. The initial exam showed you to have a fever of 104°, and you were bleeding from multiple wounds, namely your legs." He pulls up the oversized sleeve of my hospital gown to look at my arm. "It's this, though, that we have the most concern. We'll get to that."

The fresh bandage on my forearm is white and clean. Gnarly red

Chapter 15

lines crawl out from under the gauze, heading up toward my shoulder. Infection, even I know that. Things were starting to make more sense, even if the memories looked like a reflection in a funhouse mirror.

"We cleaned you up, started an IV with a broad-spectrum antibiotic, and got you settled in this room. Now your temperature has dropped to normal, and those lines have markedly decreased in tone and length. As long as the trend continues in the right direction, you should be out of here before dinnertime." As a lame attempt at a joke, he warns me, "Meatloaf is on the menu. You want to be as far away as possible.

"As far as the other injuries, they look okay. If you had bandaged them, they wouldn't be so irritated."

I contradict him. "They were. I can remember the stickiness of the tape bothering me. I might have taken the scabs with the Band-aids when I tore them off."

"When did you initially hurt yourself?"

"A week ago."

"Well, that explains that. The cuts looked fresh when you arrived. The problem was, you missed a small piece of a stick in your arm. It festered and caused all this trouble. We got it out and had to debride a small amount of flesh from around it. We didn't use sutures to prevent further aggravation, just a few butterfly bandages. Please keep it clean and covered until a good scab can form. Any questions?"

"So, I wasn't kidnapped." It's not a question. I owe my buddies a huge favor.

"No." The doctor laughs with his whole face. I like his bedside manner. "Those guys took more flak from you than I usually see. You're a fighter, and, in this case, that's a good thing. It would have been a bad situation if they hadn't happened upon you. Luckier still, after carrying you for a mile, they were able to contact a friend of a friend." He refers back to the notes. "Becky. She picked you all up and drove you over here. I'll leave her number. She said she could drive you to where you end up staying."

A trail angel. *You gotta love 'em!*

"Do you have any idea why they tied me up? I mean, that doesn't make sense."

He pauses for a moment, then recalls. "Ah! Hold on a sec." Moments later, he's back. "Does this look familiar?" The doctor holds up a thin, army-green camouflage nylon fabric.

"My poncho liner. I use it instead of a sleeping bag now that it's so warm."

"The group had you wrapped in it. They were trying to multi-task, from what the charge nurse told us. You were bleeding, struggling, and getting the chills. You'll get the rest of your gear with the discharge papers." He hands me the bedding, and the smell of the trail clinging to its fibers fills me with homesickness. I lay it over the hospital blanket, not for the warmth but the moral support.

"It's customary with such a high fever for things not to make sense. Some of it will come back to you, but a lot will stay gone completely or seem too weird for reality.

"We'll be sending you out with a prescription for oral antibiotics. Take them religiously, and you'll be fine. Also, don't do anything strenuous, including backpacking, for at least two more days. If you have no fever on Wednesday and you feel strong, you can head out and finish the meds on the trail." He pauses to add some final notes before closing his laptop. "Never saw the appeal of walking such long distances personally, but I treat enough of you hikers to know I'm not going to be able to stop you from doing it yourself."

I ignore the remark.

"Does that about cover it, Jordan?"

"Do you know the number to a local hotel or hostel?"

"Dial zero." He points to an old rotary phone on the bedside table. "Mary will hook you up with all that information. Then rest." He gives me a severe look. "If you want to reach the top of Mount Katahdin, follow all my advice. Good luck."

"Thanks, Doc."

16

JORDAN

Becky picks me up at the curb after a gruelingly long wait for discharge from the hospital. As Dr. Matthews promised, they called in my prescription already. All I need to do is check into the hotel and relax after obtaining it, along with a few other provisions. Less achy than earlier, it's now exhaustion that overwhelms me. Tomorrow I will focus on some mind and bodywork to enhance healing, but tonight I need sleep.

"Hi, Jordan!" Becky chirps, enthusiastically. She's younger and more animated than I remember. Maybe twenty, her face carries the residual effects of teen years spent battling acne, though it hardly detracts from her bubbly cuteness. She strikes me as a late bloomer, and I cross my fingers that her journey toward full blossom isn't too challenging. Earnestness seeps through her every move and phrase. I know that attitude is a magnet for users. "How are you? Where would you like to go first? I'm sorry I can't have you stay at my place. Parents, you know?" Becky blushes as she inhales deeply, replacing the oxygen she lost from her verbal release.

"Becky, I can't thank you enough." I squeeze her hand once before adjusting my seat belt. "If I had the strength, I'd host you tonight so you could have a taste of freedom."

She puts the car in drive and pulls into the light traffic, smiling shyly.

"But I'm about to collapse, so if we could hit the pharmacy and maybe a drive-thru, that would be great."

My trail angel does me so much better. First, she picks up the medication, so I can sit in her air-conditioned car. Next, we go to the supermarket. List in hand, she buys everything I could crave in the next forty-eight hours and then some. Finally, Becky orders from the best restaurant in town instead of a drive-thru meal. And by best, I mean the most considerable portions: a thick, juicy steak, a baked potato, a side salad—breadsticks included—and dessert. In less than an hour, she has become my new best friend.

Pulling her small car into the drop-off vestibule at the hotel, I wonder how I'll get my cache upstairs when she pops the trunk, shuts down the engine, and hops out. I guess Becky is how.

"Come on. I'll help you check-in."

Arms laden, we approach the main desk. A young man immersed in his phone looks up and smiles wonkily at Becky. "Hey, Bex." He sounds stoned but has an extremely handsome face.

Becky's face flames as she fusses around. Shuffling her feet, hiding my dinner sack behind her back, she manages to squeak out, "Hi, Todd."

I roll my eyes. Heaven forbid your crush thinks you eat. They do make a cute couple, though.

"Hey," he repeats.

Recognizing this scintillating back and forth could continue for a while, I break in. "Yeah, okay. Hi, Todd." I wave to get his attention.

He looks at me tiredly. "Hey." A man of few words, the spark he had for Becky, he doesn't share with paying guests.

"I'd like to check-in before I collapse."

My request spurs Becky into action. "Oh! Yes. Right. Um. Jordan has a room booked here. Tonight."

If I weren't tired enough to cry, I would laugh at how difficult it was for her to string a complete sentence together.

"Okay." Todd types for an interminably long time on the keyboard

Chapter 16

until he finally hands me the access card. "Room 202 is on the second floor. Take a right off the elevator. Continental breakfast is in that room, starting at seven o'clock."

He points to a small dark space that I will not be entering even in the daylight. The drop tile is stained brown from an apparent leak in the ceiling, and someone has left a big red bucket on the floor underneath. The coffee urn is held together with duct tape, and it appears the fare offered consists only of cellophane-wrapped sugar bombs. Spying a coffee cake variety with vanilla frosting and cinnamon crumbles, I decide to keep my options open. There is no reason for snobbery.

"Great." I gather my goods and head to the elevator with Becky right behind me.

"Sorry. That was Todd." She blushes again, her face sunny with a thousand-watt smile.

"I gathered." Her crush is adorable. I hope he doesn't break her heart.

She tells me all about him as we head up to the room. "He was in my science class in tenth grade, and then we took a writing class together at the local community college. Well, not just us. Other students were there. And a teacher. Back in high school, he asked me to dance at the spring fling. I said no because I can't dance, but he asked, which means something, right? Then, last semester, he borrowed a pen. He gave it back, and I still have it. I keep it in my memory box so that my mom doesn't touch it. It has his fingerprints on it, so, you know."

I know I need her to shut up and go away, but I also need to be kind, as she did me a massive solid. So I break into her speech, hoping it will help me get into the gigantic king-size bed sooner rather than later. "I understand, Becky. You're in love and afraid. You know what you should do?"

Her eyes are as big as saucers from my mind-reading as she whispers, "No. What?"

"Go ask him out. Put fear aside, go downstairs, and just say it."

"Say what?" She really is clueless. I suppose most of us are at her age.

"Whatever you'd like to do. 'Hey, Todd, maybe we could go out to dinner? Take in a movie? A walk in the park?' Ask whatever you think the both of you would enjoy. What do you have to lose?"

She thinks deeply before answering, "Pride?"

I wave her answer away. "It comes back, trust me. You'll regret not asking. If Todd says no, it will sting at first, but down the road, you'll be glad you did it anyway. Do it, Becky. Do it because you're awesome. Do it because you're only young once." I can't tell her my darker truth. *Do it because I'm selfish and tired, and my threshold for enthusiasm has been tapped.* So instead, I add, "Do it right now."

My pep talk works. Becky is clapping her hands and bouncing on her heels. "You're right. I'm going to walk straight up to Todd and ask him out."

I hand her a piece of paper with my contact information. "Here. Take this. You call or text me anytime, anywhere, for any reason. I owe you, Becky. You've been a lifesaver."

She pulls me into a bear hug. "Thank you, Jordan. I'll never forget this night. And you don't owe me anything. Trail angels just ask that you pay it forward."

How sweet is she?

"Let me know how everything goes, okay?"

Too excited to speak, she squeals as I close the door in her face.

17

JORDAN

I'm rested but lazy as hell. The bed is littered with empty chip bags and chocolate wrappers as I tune into morning talk shows. Maybe it's the months being on the trail where the only TV time I get is at the laundromat, but the content seems more foolish than ever. The hosts hardly look human with all the Botox and enhancement surgeries, and the guests are there as sycophants and sounding boards for the day's agenda.

I dream of coffee during commercials, but that would entail putting on a bra and facing the world. I'm not so uncivilized that I would drink the bathroom coffee the hotel provides, so instead, I roll over to catch another forty winks.

Just as I slip into oblivion, someone knocks at the door.

I forgot to put up the "Do Not Disturb" sign for housekeeping and call out, "I'm all set. Thanks."

"Jordan?" A recognizable voice inquires from beyond.

Instantly wide awake, I scoot from the bed and take in my surroundings. Forget the wrappers; everything I own is tossed helter-skelter. Clothes, draped over chairs, are drying by the air conditioner. My camping gear is strewn, awaiting orderly packing when I'm all set to go. I do it that way so as not to forget anything. I'm a visual gal.

Somehow my Ampicillin bottle toppled over, and fat, yellow pills spill over the bedside table. It looks like a drug addict spent the night on a bender. Before opening the door, the last thing I spy, nestled between the bed pillows, is the take-out container from my steak dinner.

Brett would have had my head over such a mess when we were together. Not that he was neat, far from it, but it was my job to put things away properly.

I reframe the state of the room in my mind. The reaction I receive will be a litmus test verifying the man's character beyond the door or indicate quickly a lack thereof.

All of my concerns about getting away with my slovenly behavior go out the window when I see Adam standing in the hall, looking neat as a pin. A drool-worthy pin. His khakis are perfectly pressed, and his green Oxford shirt is wrinkle-free and neatly rolled up to the elbows, exposing his muscular, deeply tanned forearms. With his killer smile, he could be on the cover of *People's* Sexiest Man Alive.

"Aren't you a sight for sore eyes," he tells me. "I was scared to death when I read your blog."

"My blog?" It's been a week since I last posted. At least, I hope so. No telling what I might have written in my feverish state. "How did you know where I was?"

"Same place. A guy named Pack Rat posted about finding you in the woods."

I balk; mortified people know of my struggles from a different source. They may have saved my ass, but it didn't give them the right to take over my life.

"He didn't make a detailed announcement or anything. Another follower, I think his name was Moonshine, got wind of it and posted you were near death. Pack Rat calmed everyone down and kept it generic. It's still a fifty-fifty split between those who believe Pack Rat and those who think you're dead."

"Great." Social media: can't live with it, can't stay connected without it. Such are the trials and tribulations of this modern world.

"My assistant is a wannabe sleuth, so I sicced her on Pack Rat. He

Chapter 17

connected Sheila with a girl named Becky, who folded like a house of cards."

"Ahh, yes. Becky is an open book." She sent me a text long after I had fallen asleep last night. I've never seen so many varieties of heart emojis in my life. She and Todd have a date this Friday night. It turns out they are both into old film noir, and *Gaslight* is playing at the Cineplex.

As far as Moonshine, his favorite thing in the world is drama. The more, the merrier. I can't hold it against him. His over-the-top personality keeps things fun and light on the trail.

I could plot revenge, but I have more pressing issues with Adam standing at the door looking incredibly edible, while I present like something chewed up and spit out. "How did you get here so fast?"

"I'm staying two towns over doing a walk-thru at the lab of a potential new client. I was packing for the airport when Sheila came through with the details."

"Impressive."

"She's a gem. No argument there."

He's still standing in the hall with two coffees and a brown paper bag in hand. Assuming the latter doesn't hold a forty for him to fit in with the junkie atmosphere I've accidentally created, it appears breakfast has arrived.

"I can't believe you went to all this trouble." I'm impressed at his thoughtfulness.

"Trouble? I only wish you had let me know yourself. I meant what I said when I dropped you off, Jordan. You call, I'll come running. Deal?"

Sounds too good to be true. *We'll see.*

I reach for the coffee at the same time Adam leans in to kiss my cheek. We both stop mid-motion. I apologize for my grabby ways while he blurts, "I thought they cleaned you up at the hospital?" If he thinks I look messy, wait until he gets a load of the room.

"That looks like blood." He points to my chin as I lead him inside, already swilling the hot beverage.

I take a look in the mirror. It's not blood. "Um, that's steak juice." I wet the edge of my t-shirt with water and wipe my chin clean. It's then I realize that I'm not wearing anything under the top. Without meaning to, I'm completely flashing him, with the mirror's help, a view of both my front and back. Tugging the shirt down, I turn to face him. "Sorry." I feel awkward and exposed. I itch to clean the room, the old habit fighting with my new resolve to do things my way, the opinion of others be damned.

"Why are you in such an apologetic mood, Jordan? You've done nothing wrong that I can see."

I feel his eyes roving my face and body. I'm afraid to look, to witness derision, but force eye contact. What I discover is concern battling with desire. "Would you like to sit on the balcony while I take a shower?"

"No." He saunters my way and tenderly cradles my face in his hands. Holding it like a treasure, he kisses me sweetly once, twice, three times, each more probing than the last. Pulling me close to his chest, his hands explore my backside. "What I want is to take a shower with you. I can rub your aching muscles and help you tend to those wounds. What do you think?"

"I think that's the best offer I've had since the carnival."

All thoughts of messy spaces fall away as he lifts me gently and carries me to the bathroom.

18

JORDAN

The shower has a surprising number of jets, each with intense, steady pressure. With the hot water cranked as high as it can go, the tightness in my muscles is already releasing its hold. I lean back with Adam supporting most of my weight against his solid chest as he works the thick lather into my scalp with his strong hands. He gives it a good rinse and massages in the conditioner before traveling down the rest of my body with his powerful fingers.

Focusing on every last inch of me, he starts with my neck and shoulders, kneads along the length and breadth of my back, and doesn't stop until he has one foot resting on his knee, forcing the stiffness from my arch. Nirvana is a loving man tenderly touching you unselfishly.

After finishing with my second foot, he heads slowly back up, focusing on my front where all the wounds are. He dribbles soap through a washcloth and dabs them so softly that I hardly feel a sting. Adam surprises me when he kisses me at the apex of my legs, causing me to gasp.

"Sorry. I couldn't resist."

Nor do I want him to. I prop my foot on the side of the bathtub as he grins salaciously up at me. No words from me are necessary. With his skill, no direction is warranted.

I'm breathless and beyond relaxed when he finishes his magic. I laugh and share, "I could not have asked for better aftercare."

"I aim to please," he promises.

After drying us both thoroughly and covering my cuts with ointment and bandages, Adam carries me back to bed. "Stay right there," he commands before heading back to the bathroom. He soon returns with the body lotion and reworks my muscles. This is no man but a god.

Before I can tell him so, I fall into a dreamless sleep.

⁕

I wake to the canned laugh track of yet another talk show. The ease in my body is apparent. Hardly an ache lingers, and my temperature feels normal. I want to get back on the trail. I'll go mad if I have to lie here and listen to this gibberish much longer. "Shut it off," I plead to Adam's back.

He's dressed again and sitting on the edge of the bed, one of the few uncluttered spaces. After a short struggle between man and foreign clicker, the noise stops. "Hey, Jordan. You're awake. Can I get you some coffee?"

"What time is it?" I'm not a good napper and tend to wake up cranky. But I can once again understand the concept of time, so there is that.

"It's two in the afternoon."

I yawn hugely. "No. I'll never sleep if I have caffeine this late. How about a walk to get some take-out?"

He lies down beside me, stroking my hair. "I can get you whatever you need."

"It might be a good idea for me to test out my strength."

Raising an eyebrow, he tells me, "I have a test for that." His hand is already sneaking under the sheet, gliding over the curve of my hip.

"Do you now?"

"Um-hm. It's pretty intense, so I suggest you let me show you what it entails. If you're up for it later, maybe you can give it a try." Angling

Chapter 18

his mouth over mine, he kisses me deeply. His hands have already found my breasts, caressing them with a feather-soft touch.

"This cover will have to go." It whisks off in an instant; the breeze from the a/c immediately goosebumps my flesh.

As he pulls one hardened nipple into his mouth, I arch my back from the sensation of hot and cold. He is a very gifted man. Adam's hand trails down my abdomen. His fingers are tracing the indent of my belly button when someone knocks at the door.

"Son of a bitch," I say and jump up to dress.

After giving Adam the go-ahead, he swings the door wide open.

It really is a son of a bitch. "What are you doing here, Brett?"

"You never disabled the GPS on your phone, so I figured you wanted me to find you. After reading what your new friends," he says the last word like an epithet, "wrote on your blog, I was worried. I had to see if you were okay. You haven't responded to my post on River Jordan." Both my blog and trail names. "I didn't realize you would already have company." He sneers at Adam as he enters the room.

Brett swoops in for a kiss and a hug while I struggle out of his clutches. "What the hell are you doing? Are you drunk?" I reach for the thermometer within the mess around the TV and recheck my temperature because my skin feels hot enough to fry an egg as I introduce the two men. "Adam, this is my ex-husband Brett. Brett, this is my good friend Adam." Speaking directly to Adam, I say, "I suspect once he's tossed the room for china plates, he'll be on his way."

Adam shrugs, not knowing what I'm referencing.

Brett waves his hands, dismissing my words. "Forget the dishes. I'm here for you, darlin'. This whole divorce thing was a mistake. Let's kiss and make up and put all this behind us."

The thermometer reads a healthy 98.6°, proof it's him and not me. "You're insane," I tell him. "Go home to your wife and leave me alone." I point in the direction of the door, hoping he'll go.

Seconds tick by like an eternity until Adam breaks the silence. "Maybe I should go."

My "no" coincides with Brett's "yes."

Clutching my head with my fingertips, I make another attempt to figure out Brett's angle for showing up. "Brett, either fill me in on what is going on or get the hell out. I'm not kidding."

He clears his throat three times in a row. He's hiding something. "I just want you back. Look, I made a mistake, okay? If it makes you feel better, I'll take the blame."

Un-freakin'-believable! "It was your fault, jackass! The whole thing. The constant demands for perfection, the belittling over my barrenness." I put the last word in air quotes. It was his favorite term, not mine, to identify what he perceived as my shortcomings. He doesn't define me, nor does my inability to conceive. "And the emotional and mental abuse." When he tries to cut in, I know to deny the accusation, I speak louder. "Yes, Brett, abuse! You are an abuser, and I woke up. I'll tell you another thing, Stacey will too if you don't grow up and act like a man.

"Let's not forget that you didn't just cheat on me. You cheated on me with my stepsister. You made your bed. Go lie in it!" I march to the door and open it wide. "Get out, now!" I don't care who hears my war-like cry.

"Be reasonable, Jordan." He continues to plead his case while trying to pull me back into the room.

Seeing Brett start to get physical, Adam springs into action. "You heard the lady. Get moving." He grabs Brett's elbow and escorts him out the door.

Always with the last word, Brett tells me, "I'm not finished with you yet," as the door slams closed.

19

JORDAN

*A*dam rubs my back in broad strokes as I work on bringing my heart rate down to a healthier level. "Did that just happen?" My head is spinning as I gulp down air.

"Strange, but true. I'm out of the loop here, but you could take a look at your blog once you feel up to it. Might find some answers there."

Reaching for my phone, I mutter, "No time like the present," and open the page to find chaos. Followers argue whether or not I'm alive while Brett and my cousin, Connie, swap vitriolic barbs. It looks as if trolls have infiltrated the page, but no, these are all real people venting their honest opinions behind a screen. I scroll back far enough to find the poem Brett left, "Annabelle Lee" by Edgar Allen Poe. Except he posted it under the heading, "Jordan Lee." Dear lord.

"It's beautiful," Adam tells me.

"Yeah. It's also plagiarism."

"You don't think he wrote it?"

I laugh. "I know he didn't. One, Brett is a boob. I'm surprised he knows what poetry is. Two, take a look at this." I show him the screen with the actual version of the poem penned by the real poet. It's a super pretty piece, but Brett changed one vital detail to make it look like his own. Even so, he hardly tried. Anyone with any knowledge of the tortured author would recognize the work. "I took a semester in college on Poe poetry. Instead of a tropical spring break that year, I visited his museum in Richmond, Virginia. The docent was an even bigger fan than me, and we spent hours after closing time exploring the man's darkness and light."

"Is your middle name Lee?"

"No. I never got one. My father thought they were superfluous." *Like my ex.* "No doubt Brett's a lazy plagiarist but a plagiarist nonetheless." My cousin posted the correct version and called him out immediately. He denied trying to take credit even though beneath the fabricated title, he typed his own name. "Looks like my cousin shut him right down, which I appreciate, but I need to get in there and clean house a bit. Give me thirty minutes?"

"Take all the time you need. I'll go rustle us up some dinner." He kisses me sensuously. Filled with promise, it leaves me wanting more.

❧

Responses come almost immediately to my new post. Followers flood the comment section with well-wishes, and the atmosphere changes to one more gracious.

I add a photo I just took with only the headboard to indicate my location. The last thing I need is the rest of the estranged people in my life showing up at the hotel door. Everyone can rest assured, I am alive and still utterly and gratefully divorced. Although I appreciate the lambasting my ex got, Brett is not the focus of this blog, and he never will be. I share a bit of what has been going on, keeping it all light and bright.

My phone rings soon after I log out, optimistic that truth and peace have been restored. It's my cousin.

"Hey, Connie. Thanks for looking out for me."

A few years older than me, Connie comes from my father's side of the family. I remember looking up to her when I was young, before my parents divorced and family gatherings were no longer a part of my

Chapter 19

life. She was old enough to wear make-up and smelled like a flower garden, in stark contrast to my tomboy-like ways. I found her fascinating and still do.

Connie and I reconnected and hit it off after my mom and dad died, within months of each other from unexpected but natural causes. As adults, the five-year age gap no longer mattered, and we became fast friends.

I haven't seen much of my other relatives in the Roberts clan, as they live all over the country, but Connie is throwing the first family reunion in a decade, with me as the guest of honor the same month that I will be passing through New Hampshire. It's another reason why failure is not an option. Seeing my extended family will be just the boost I need when I find myself exhausted and a state away from the finish line.

"Thank God you're okay. You had us so worried."

"Sorry. I wasn't myself, as you can imagine, or I would have called. I can't believe how quickly news travels and how convoluted everything got. It's like a game of telephone gone rogue."

"I hope I wasn't out of line with Brett. He makes my teeth itch. If I knew you when you met him, I would have seen that version of hell coming a mile away."

"You can be as out of line with him as you want. He just showed up at my hotel. Care to guess why?"

"Psh. I don't need to guess. Are you sitting down? I may leave you with the impression your ex-husband is even worse than you thought."

"Impossible, but do go on." I brace myself for impact as I lie down, resting my arm across my screen-weary eyes.

"Things got pretty interesting during labor and delivery."

"Whose?"

"Keep up, Jordan," she razzes me. "Brett and Stacey."

"Weren't they planning a home birth? Isn't the baby premature?"

"Things don't always go as planned, do they? And two weeks isn't technically early, so the baby is completely healthy. She's eight pounds, twenty-one inches, with a name you wouldn't wish on your worst enemy."

She pauses to take a breath before continuing. "Anyway, a man named Peter Parker burst into the room just as Prada Cartier was crowning. He claimed to be the biological father and demanded a DNA test. The nurses called security, but it was Brett who conceded. He walked out with barely a word and hasn't been heard from since. Well, except for the poem written on your blog."

"Ah. I feel so special. I wonder, is it the fact he can't match his socks or open a refrigerator door that has him missing me?" I snap my fingers, sitting up. "Wait! It must be because he can't bear to be alone with his horrid self for more than five minutes. I can't believe it, but you're right. Brett just ratcheted down another level in my estimation. What a horror show."

"The hospital scene?" Connie asks.

"The man," I retort, giving us both a chuckle. "By the way, are you suggesting my stepsister was hooking up with Spiderman?"

"I know, right? They posted pics on her Facebook page. He's cute in the same superficial way Brett is. I'm sure they'll be happy for a short while. Then, who knows?"

"Who cares?"

We answer at the same time, "Nobody!"

Becoming more serious, Connie asks, "Are you okay? It is such a shitty thing for him to keep playing with you after finalizing the divorce."

"I am. I have no intention of taking Brett back, regardless of why he asked. I'll still come out on top if I get nothing more from this hiking experience because life is great without drama. Good luck to all the players in this game because I, for one, have officially tapped out."

"I am so proud of you. You continue to heal, and I'll keep your ex at bay on your blog."

"Thank you. I'm so lucky to have you in my corner."

"You sure are!" Ending with another laugh, she hangs up to check in on her husband and kids.

Chapter 19

Adam still hasn't come back, even though it's been well over an hour. I want to think he's giving me space, but I worry he has simply vanished. I wouldn't blame him. Baggage might be inevitable at our age, but dealing with some random guy's histrionics is a choice.

Hoping I'm wrong, I grab the key card and head out to find him.

Todd is once again handling the front desk. His bloodshot eyes don't fill me with optimism that he would remember Adam even if he spontaneously combusted in front of him. He would probably just use the flame to light another joint.

"Hey," he says in the way of a greeting. "Thanks, man. I've liked Becky for a while. Thanks for hooking us up." He gives me the hang ten sign, eyelids at half-mast. At least he's polite.

"You're welcome. Be good to her, you hear me?"

"Totally."

Oh lord! It'll be fine. "Well, good. Tell me, did you see a tall man with dark hair, wearing khakis and a button-down shirt, leave about an hour ago?"

He thinks for longer than I would otherwise expect. When it seems I've lost him to the ether filling his headspace, he finally answers, "About ten of them. Some sort of golfing thing. Sorry."

I can't say I didn't know I would be wasting time asking. "Thanks anyway."

He grins lazily. "No problem."

When I turn to go, he calls me back. "Wait. There was a guy. Hold up." He rustles through some papers on the desk.

I hold onto my patience by eying the breakfast room for leftover snack cakes, but this was getting tedious.

"Here it is." Todd hands me a wrinkled envelope.

Expecting a Dear John, or more specifically a Dear Jordan letter, instead, I read another stolen poem in my ex-husband's scrawl. This time he chose Elizabeth Barrett Browning. Was he joking? Crumpling up the post-it note, I toss it in the trash bin on my way out. I leave any thoughts of Brett with it when I spy Adam sitting over by the small duck pond to the parking lot's right.

He stayed.

I smile.

"Hey," he says in a gentle voice. "Everything okay?"

"Yes." I fill him in on the unsavory details. He makes the right noises at the right moments, but I still feel he's distancing himself in some way. "I know it all seems so strange. It is for me, too, believe it or not. I would never have imagined half of this. But," I put a stress on the word to collect my thoughts and let him know he has the out I'm offering. "I can understand how you would want to step away from it all. It must strike you as sordid and sick. If it helps, I'm not at all related to my stepsister. She is the daughter of my father's second wife. Probably bad enough, but..." I trail off. I don't know what else to say.

We sit watching the ducks bob peacefully. Mom has her head tucked under a wing while the vibrant, green-headed dad feeds and stays alert to any threats to his five yellow ducklings.

Adam breaks the silence. "Again, you haven't done anything wrong. If anything, I hold you in even greater regard. How anyone could be so careless with your heart is beyond me. I haven't known you long, but do you think I would be here if you hadn't already made an impact on me? I like you more than anyone I've ever met.

"Your ex-husband should want you back. You're wonderful. He's a fool, and I suspect your stepsister isn't much better. Correct me if I'm wrong. I don't want to get in between family, but they certainly don't seem in the habit of being kind to you, and that is something I don't like about them."

I rarely cry, but his words have me tearing up. I blame the fever, even if it's long gone. That has to be it. I can't be getting soft. I'm a thru-hiker, and I have hundreds of miles left to complete.

He pulls me close and hands me a paper napkin to dry my cheeks. "Where did you get this?"

"I had an ice cream cone."

"Without me?" I joke, trying to lighten the atmosphere.

"Yes, Jordan. People sometimes eat even when you aren't." He gives me a big smile to buffer his offensive words. "Which reminds me, I bet dinner is ready to be picked up. I ordered you three of everything from the Italian place around the corner. That ought to hold you."

Chapter 19

"Har. Har."

"So, are we good?" He tilts my chin up, and I kiss his sensuous lips. Relief flows through me as he kisses me back. I was so afraid Brett was going to wreck this too.

"Very good."

He kisses me again, exploring the recesses of my mouth. His tongue makes me want to forget dinner and head directly back upstairs. Before I can suggest it, he stands and pulls me close. After a too-short hug and a final peck, he leads me to the restaurant to satisfy at least one of my appetites.

20

JORDAN

"'Parting is such sweet sorrow.'"

I clamp my hand over Adam's mouth as he sweeps an arm high in the air, adding a theatrical flair to his soliloquy.

"Please say it isn't so. I was afraid Brett's condition might be contagious." I grab his hand, holding it dramatically against my chest. "Tell me who wrote the words that just flowed so elegantly from your dignified tongue?"

Sandy, the Uber driver, looks at us like we're insane as she takes my backpack out of the Escalade's rear seat. After leaving me at the trailhead, she'll be taking Adam straight to the airport. We won't see each other until Massachusetts. A month ago, that seemed like forever to wait. With the extra zeros to make up for, I have to hustle to compensate for the lost time.

"Why, Juliet, don't you know? They are from me, Romeo. Your ill-fated lover!" He swoops me down, the ends of my hair touch the dirt, and kisses me deeply.

Sandy makes a lot of noise, opening and closing doors, interrupting the moment.

"Sorry," we both say as he lifts me back to stand. We express our goodbyes like the grownups we are, instead of poor excuses for Shakespearean stage actors.

"I'll miss you," he tells me.

"Me too."

"You call me anytime, day or night, that anything even remotely threatening happens to you. I mean, if a coyote howls in the distance, I want to know."

"I don't think so," I tell him lovingly, but honestly.

When he objects, I clarify. "I promise to tell you if something big like this happens again. Anything that will keep me off-trail, I'll share. Everything else is mine alone." I'm crazy possessive now about this experience. At first, I was excited, often daunted, and now? I'm obsessed. I love every moment, the ups, downs, and all-around's.

"You drive a hard bargain, but okay. Please stay safe and know I'm thinking of you and rooting for your continued success."

"Aww. Thanks, Adam." With a final kiss goodbye, we separate our hands, and I disappear down the path.

ADAM

I want to relive the last couple of days spent with Jordan to pass the time going home, but my phone rings instead.

"Hi, Sheila. I'm heading to the airport now."

"Good for you," she tells me without feeling. "There's trouble brewing here."

It's always something. I wonder if I'm too old for the rat race. I like my work, but lately, it's been more of a grind than anything. I've been running the show for so long that I find myself missing the excitement of starting new and creating something from nothing. The job is a cash cow, but my satisfaction level is at an all-time low.

"What is it?"

"It's your boy, Jonathan, up to no good. If it were up to me, I'd have kicked him out long ago. Nothing but trouble, that one."

Jonathan has consistently been a loose cannon. He likes to make sweeping executive decisions, often forgetting the senior partner and board of directors he needs to consider. Jonathan is sexist and rude and has never believed in a set schedule for himself. But he does hold the second largest number of shares, and he is an incredible accountant.

"What did he do now?"

"He accepted the offer from Phased Vision."

"What?" I virtually explode out of the front seat as we pull up to the airport check-in. I tip Sandy as she hands me my overnight bag. I mouth "thank you" and enter the building. "We voted 10-3 for Dynamic Design, contingent on what I found on the lab tour. When did this happen?"

"An hour ago, Cindy Gregg walked out of his office, a triumphant smile and smudged lipstick on her face. Worse, Kim stopped by with the baby. She must have passed the vile woman in the hall and left Jonathan's office in tears within minutes of arriving. She flew past me on her way out, bordering on hysteria, and refused a ride home. He's a piece of work, I gotta say." She clicks her tongue in what I feel is a personal slight. "If I recall correctly, I did warn you." She confirms my impression, and I know it to be true.

"Get everyone on the board and the lawyers together. I'll be there in less than three hours. No one leaves, understood?"

"Got it, boss. Should I order dinner?"

"Yes, it's going to be a late night. But don't include me." I can never eat when things blow up at work. It seems an extravagance.

"I know."

That's it. No more. Either Jonathan goes, or I do. Not knowing which choice would be better for the company at this point, I call my close confidant and personal attorney, Clint. I know he will advise me well, maybe even sit in on the upcoming meeting.

※

"Clint." I greet him with a handshake before we head up to the boardroom together. He never was one to get caught up in rules, prefer-

Chapter 20

ring to march to the beat of his own drum. It was his old-fashioned ways that made me hire him fifteen years ago. He reminds me of my dad, who believed a man's handshake was equivalent to his word. In this day and age where handshakes are verboten, society still has yet to find a similar sign to replace it. I consider myself lucky to know someone like Clint and haven't regretted a single decision in which he has taken part.

"Adam. How are you? This situation with Jonathan could get sticky. But I've got a solid plan ready, depending on how all this goes down."

I knew he wouldn't fail me. "Great. I'm hoping people will be as shocked as I am, and it will go smoother than we think. Odds on that?" Not a betting man myself, I'm sure he won't offer a wager.

"Pshaw. Sixty-forty, if the Fates are on your side." He presses the elevator button as he talks. "People don't like change. It's against their nature, but the evidence is there. I think we have to be willing to pay through the nose. Otherwise, Jonathan could drag this through court for years. Whoever brokered his contract did a great job."

"I was afraid of that. We'll have to see."

"I'll just observe, and we'll strategize if need be once all is said and done."

Clint hangs his Stetson hat on the coat rack, keeps a hold of his briefcase, and takes a seat in a dimly lit corner. You can hardly tell he's in the room.

I sit down and check to see if I have any texts from Jordan. What I wouldn't give to have us both still at the hotel. The screen is blank, so I turn my attention to Sheila's arrival. She gives me a curt nod while Clint gets a beaming smile. Sheila hates to work late but has always been able to put her feelings aside for Clint, while I'm sure to hear more of her frustrations about Jonathan before going home tonight.

Within minutes the rest of the team is present and ready to go, laptops open. One key person is missing: Jonathan. Not willing to wait, I stand to get their attention. "Thank you for coming on short notice. You know I don't call these meetings casually, so I'll get right to the point."

Jonathan strolls in as if he owns the place, casually greeting a few people he considers friends. It's fascinating and sad how blatant his dismissal of me is. I wonder how long it has been since he considered me his friend. I've become so used to his surly and crude behavior that I overlooked the foundation we had built upon since childhood has crumbled to an irreparable state.

"Glad you could join us, Jonathan. Maybe you should open up the meeting."

Standing directly to my left, I hear him mumble, "About time."

I nonchalantly wave, as I sit back down, giving him the floor. "Please, fill everyone in on why we're here."

"I met with the CEO of Phased Vision and accepted their bid." He looks proud as a peacock while the rest of the table explodes into unintelligible objections. He puts up his hands to calm the noise. "I know. I know. Most of you voted for Dynamic Design, but it made no sense. They cost three times as much. From a financial standpoint, I had to save you from yourselves."

Clint gestures discreetly from the corner. Instead of responding, I sit back and watch the ensuing chaos. So far, so good. Everyone is up in arms against Jonathan's decision.

Reggie chimes in the loudest. "You had no right! You went behind all our backs. When is it going to stop?"

Jean is next. "You are disgusting. I should have reported you to human resources years ago after your behavior at the Christmas party. I don't think everyone here knows why you chose Phased Vision. Shall I tell them?"

"Jean, calm down." Jonathan's smile is condescending, and his input does nothing to settle the woman's ire.

Kevin holds her back from lunging over the table. "You've always been a bad fit," Kevin tells him as he gingerly hands Jean a bottle of water. It appears as if fraternizing might be more rampant than I thought. Everyone on the board signed a contract forbidding it with staff from other companies and underlings. In the case of Kevin and Jean, they are all set, being equals. I wish them all the luck.

"He fucked her!" Jean yells out.

Chapter 20

The room goes silent as jaws drop before rising to a crescendo even louder than what it was after Jonathan made his shocking announcement. Things have unraveled a lot faster than I ever expected. Having no other choice, I step in. "Okay, everyone. Please, let's take our seats for a moment and collect ourselves."

Jean flips Jonathan the bird before sitting down. Kevin speaks quietly in her ear until a small smile appears. Two people are going to vote on the right side.

Fingers fly over cell phones, communicating with the person beside them, across the table, and possibly beyond the doors. I warn everyone, "What happens in the boardroom, stays in the boardroom."

I allow a solid five minutes to pass before speaking again. "Jonathan, you have broken numerous company rules and, more specifically, clauses that violate your contract with the company. First thing tomorrow, I will be canceling the deal you made with Phased Vision, and I will be accepting the bid from Dynamic Design. I expect your letter of resignation on my desk by eight tomorrow morning."

"You won't be getting it!" he yells as he erupts from his chair. "You haven't even brought it to a vote." He's pacing like a tiger, red-faced, but I've witnessed his bluff too many times to give it much attention.

His funeral, I think. Because no way will this group tolerate his despicable behavior any longer.

"I don't need a vote, Jonathan. You broke your contract multiple ways. But, I'll humor you. Let's cast our ballots, people. Vote 'yea,' and Jonathan submits his resignation. Vote 'nay,' and we'll put a case together to have him removed from his role." I nod at the two company lawyers by my side. They know the deal.

It takes less than a minute for my phone to rack up the tally. Eleven members want his resignation tendered ASAP, and two want things done the hard way. The oddball out, our newest member, Kait, voted with Jonathan.

I look down at the last chair and see her mooning over the angry man. When she catches me watching, she blushes furiously and begins to tap mindlessly on her computer. I never noticed how much she resembles Kim. I send Sheila a quick text. After casting a dirty look in

Kait's direction, she sends me a thumbs-up emoji. My detective is on the case. I should know before long if Jonathan has a distant admirer or something more intimate with our group's newest member.

"So there it is. You broke the contract, you got voted off, and you will submit your resignation tomorrow morning." And with that, I announce the meeting adjourned. After my hand signal, two burly security guards walk into the room and wait by the only exit door.

"Fine. But you'll regret this. Every one of you." Jonathan collects his things, glaring at everyone except Kait. Too bad. She had excellent references and a stellar resume, but she'll soon follow my erstwhile friend out the door.

His threat is too late. I already regret ever getting into this venture with Jonathan. I always knew deep down he wasn't to be trusted, but he was my oldest friend. He was fun, the brashest guy at any college party. He had the kind of personality you wanted to be around when the beer was flowing, and the music was blaring. Unfortunately, it's been the polar opposite with him here at work. Sure, he's a math savant, but he's disrespectful and has turned into a cad of the worst type.

He pushes past security, the glass door shuddering in protest of the wide swing, and takes the stairs instead of waiting for the elevator. It looks like a police pursuit with the two guards hot on his heels. They have their orders. He gets thirty minutes to pack his things, and I get his computer.

Something stinks in Denmark, and I don't think it's merely the inappropriate affiliations.

21

JORDAN

"Jordan?" Over the phone, Kim breaks the silence around me, her voice thick and raspy. "Are you alone?"

"Hey," I answer in the hushed tone I tend to use on the trail, especially when I'm communicating with the great beyond. "I was just talking to my mom, so, yeah." She doesn't tell me I'm nuts, so I know something is amiss. "Are you okay?"

"No! It's Jonathan." She's crying so hard I can barely make out the words.

"What is it?" I find a thick-trunked tree to lean against that's perfect for sitting and listening. I remove my pack, finally light and free, and use it to prop my feet up as I lounge. A wave of guilt washes over me for the pleasure the relaxing pose brings. What if he's dead?

"I caught him with another woman." She's on the brink of hysteria by the sound of it. "He had sex with her at work."

"Oh!" I try to act surprised, but I'm not. Jonathan always had that vibe about him. Even though he was with Kim, he was always looking for something else. Jonathan was grossly overt when looking at other women and barely paid any mind to anything Kim had to say. When going out with friends, he would forget to call if he'd be late. Sometimes Jonathan failed to come home, period. I always imagined he was doing something more than drinking too much alcohol on those nights. If he upgraded to risking his career to get laid at work, I think my suspicions are confirmed.

"Oh no, Kim. I'm so sorry. Do you want to talk about it?"

"Yes," she all but hisses. "She's the CEO of some company they're hiring. Can you believe that?"

"I remember Adam checking out the place, but I didn't know they had decided on a specific one yet."

"Jordan! That is so not the point."

"Right, yes. Sorry. I'm deflecting because this is so terrible." I disagree with my words. She is much better off without him. "What are you going to do?"

"I don't know. When I came home after catching him, I threw Jonathan's suits out the window." She lets out a devilish little laugh. "Right before the pool guy came, in they all went, including the wool Armani. I watched as he fished them out, leaving a pile by the pool house. Jonathan came home, late again, and carried the dripping mess to his car. I bet he had Mommy take them all to the dry cleaners for him."

"Is that where he's staying?"

His mother was a peach. Molly probably spoiled him too much growing up, but she does the same to everybody, Kim's friends included. I had the flu once and remembered thinking it would be worth getting that sick again to taste her chicken noodle soup one more time. She brought me buckets full, along with tissues and ginger ale and loads of magazines to read while I recovered.

"I have no idea. Probably. I bet Molly is cleaning his room and cooking him all his meals too. I sometimes wish she wasn't so nice."

"I know. Jonathan doesn't deserve it. I think you made the right choice."

"You do?" Her broken little girl's voice is heart-wrenching.

"I do. You need time to process this and get your head on straight. You need more information and probably some input from friends."

"Yeah. That's why I called you first. You've been here."

"Yup. You're not alone." I sneak bites of granola and sips of water

Chapter 21

between sympathetic sounds without being obvious. My body is used to eating whenever it's not in motion, and I fear the gurgling would be a distraction.

"I know-w-w!" Kim whines, going off on another crying jag. She blows her nose, sounding like a goose under duress, before continuing. "What about Liam? I don't want him to grow up without a father."

"He won't." I roll my eyes, grateful she can't see me. He's a shitty role model, but Liam will have to make do, I guess. "No matter what happens, Jonathan will always be his father."

Kim turns on me like a viper. "Like you know anything about it! You never had a baby with Brett."

"Whoa! Cool your jets there." We shared a dorm room through college, so I know how she gets. Lashing out is part of the way she processes and grieves. It doesn't mean I'm going to be a doormat about it. I'm not listening to any more subtle digs about my inability to procreate from anyone, not even my best friend. "I'm just trying to be supportive."

She takes a thin, reedy breath and apologizes. "I'm sorry. I'm not thinking straight. When can you get here?"

"October?"

"Darn. I knew that." She sighs deeply. "I better go. I've got to wake Liam from his nap, or he'll never sleep tonight. I'll keep you posted, okay?"

Already regretting what I was about to suggest, I say, "You know, I planned to see Adam in Massachusetts. Why don't you fly up and see me instead?"

"I can't ask you to do that." Her tone indicates she's battling between her answer and the desire to have a friend by her side.

"You didn't ask. I offered. It'll be like old times. What do you say?"

"I say yes! When do you think you'll arrive?" She sounds happier now.

"We didn't nail that part down. Adam was going to book everything."

"I can do it. I'll get you a ride, find a hotel, whatever we need. You pick the dates." I can hear her tapping away, already searching on the computer. "Thank you. I'm sorry I got ornery."

"Don't be. It's part of your charm." I'm able to leave her with a laugh.

Adam

"It's Adam. Talk to me." I have no time for pleasantries these days. The fallout from Jonathan's indiscretion has been a fiasco. The lawyers are busy working their magic to get us out of the seedy deal between Phased Vision and us while I broker a valid contract with Dynamic Design.

I turn away from my computer screen and rub my face. Knowing I should take more breaks away from this thing, I keep my eyes closed as the caller speaks.

"Okay. What would you like me to say?"

I expected to hear my assistant's voice. Instead, it's Jordan's sexy sound, an octave lower than usual. Wanting to know how far she's willing to go with this, I advise, "Start with what you're wearing."

"Creepy," she whispers provocatively. "Do you happen to drive a van?"

I'm laughing for what feels like the first time in a while.

She continues filling my request. "Shorts, caked in mud. A tank top with wide, oval-shaped sweat stains under my arms, around my breasts, and sticking to the small of my back. Socks so dirty, I can smell them even when I'm standing, and a recently restocked backpack determined to break my spine. Want some of this, big boy?" She performs a great Marilyn impression at the end with her breathy voice, but she has no future in being a phone sex maven. Another good reason the industry should go the way of the dodo.

Still, I play along. "Mmm. Do you smell as bad as the day we met?"

Chapter 21

With a throaty chuckle, she wantonly whispers, "Worse. So much worse."

"Okay, you win." I can hear her clap as the phone slips from her grasp. It sounds like it lands in a pile of leaves.

"Sorry." I hear her wipe the phone clean. "There's no easy way to say this, but I can't meet you in Massachusetts."

"Oh, no!" I'm sorely disappointed, then immediately worried. "Are you okay? Is it your arm? Brett?"

"No. But now that you bring it up, life has been rather theatrical for a woman living in the woods. Kim and Jonathan separated."

"I know. The board fired Jonathan."

"Hm. Kim didn't mention that part."

"Yeah. Technically, we let him resign, but we didn't give him a choice, so." I am unsure of how much I can say. Considering my contract and Jordan and Kim being friends, I don't offer any details.

Sheila made good on her detective work. Not only were Kait and Jonathan fooling around, but Jonathan is also staying at her place. The day after the meeting, I received both resignations, making things easier for the company and Sheila.

"Yikes. Well, I'm no Jonathan fan, but I am trying to support Kim. She needs a friend, so I told her she could have my free days. I know this makes me sound like a jerk, as though I'm picking her over you. Even worse, you gave me a place to stay when I needed one, and now I'm doing this."

I let her ramble her apology, thinking it probably makes her feel better.

"I'm sorry, Adam, but she needs me."

"You're wonderful," I tell her, even though the turn of events is disappointing.

"Aww, thanks! I didn't expect you to have that reaction."

"You're a good friend. I get it. However, you're going to have to make it up to me." I tease.

"Yes! I will do that." Jordan pauses for a moment, then asks, "But how?"

"Do you have any more zeros hidden away?"

"No. I mean, I'm staying with my cousin for two days in New Hampshire for a family reunion, but I'm feeling the pinch from my other stops. I still have plenty of time to make it, but only if I stick to the program and nothing significant happens."

"Then, I'll have to get a van and meet you on the side of the road somewhere."

"Gross! Do you know how sick and twisted that sounds?" She's laughing, but in an "I laugh, so I don't freak out" kind of way.

"You started it," I tease her back.

"True. I do owe you one."

"What about Katahdin?" The truth is, with everything so sideways, it's probably for the best we don't meet in Massachusetts. It just doesn't feel that way at all right now.

"What about it?"

"How about if I meet you there? I'll take you from the mountaintop to anywhere you want to go."

"Yes! That's a wonderful idea. But, wait. Wouldn't that mean I owe you again?"

"Maybe," I tell her playfully. "Would that be so bad?"

"Would it be anything like when you were my caretaker or when we went swimming?" Her sultry voice is back, and this time, I like what she's saying.

"Just like that, only more so."

"Then double yes. I look forward to taking my time paying you back, Adam."

I groan, already picturing the fun we'll have. It will be bitter cold in Maine by then. I imagine us at a ski lodge, bundled up in warm blankets by a fire, sipping wine while we watch the snowfall. Or maybe she'll want us to fly away to somewhere warm. I envision a hot beach and gauze-covered tiki huts with nothing more than swimsuits to clothe us day in and day out. Either or. Here or there. Anywhere with Jordan is the only place I want to be.

"Keep being safe, beautiful."

"Bye, Adam."

22

JORDAN

"River!" A man calls my name from within the thicket to my right, rushing closer as he calls out again. "Stop!"

Twigs snap, and the underbrush crushes as he stumbles onto the path. Moonshine yanks me into a bear hug so strong the trekking poles I tucked in my pack dig grooves into my back from the pressure.

"Dammit, Moonshine, don't!" I laugh as I push him off. He greets everyone the same way. Woe to the day hiker who gets in front of him. Stranger, friend, foe, everyone is a target for his enthusiasm. He gets away with it because of his childlike attitude and curly mop of blonde hair. Moonshine prides himself on maintaining a high level of hygiene on the trail. He is always freshly shorn and wastes precious pack space with a shaving kit stuffed with extravagances like an entire bar of soap, aftershave, and condoms. Plus mascara. He says those baby blues have got to pop. While fit as a gladiator, Moonshine likes his luxuries.

"I can't help it. You're just who I wanted to see. Prettiest lady on the trail." He's a big-time flirt too. "Have some free time in your schedule?"

Not sure where he's going with this, I shrug. "Maybe."

"Great." As usual, he takes everything as a yes. "Stoner, Beckon,

Ash, and Phoenix aren't far behind. They're gathering more people as they go. A-Z and Quark are at least a mile ahead. They're in charge of the provisions. We'll handle camp setup. You in?"

"Can you be more specific?" He wraps his arm around my shoulders, knocking us off balance, and I hit a tree with my hip.

"Get off me, beast." I shove him playfully to the other side of the path, about six inches away.

"Can't you put two and two together?" He's gesticulating madly. "We're having a party! Remember when you were a kid, and you'd head into the woods with a bunch of friends and drink and carouse and get arrested and spend the weekend in lock up and go home to find your parents had all the locks changed, and you spend the next week couch surfing from friend to friend to friend. Or," he speaks out of the side of his mouth, "older gentlemen, to a hotter gentleman, to a richer gentleman." He elbows me in the side. "Am I right?"

"Um, no. That memory seems to have slipped my mind."

My trail friend had a tough time growing up. His parents weren't cruel, per se, but it sure looked that way on paper. Adopting a tough-love stance on Moonshine's behaviors, they thought they were helping. Instead, it put him in a lot of danger. Lucky for him, one of the men who offered him a couch was a member of the Boys and Girls Club of America. He helped Moonshine accept himself just as he was, enabling him to be a shining light ever since.

I love the end of his story. He can't fool me, though. The residual pain still reflects in his eyes. I suppose it's his "why" for being on the trail. Like many of us thru-hikers, it's our stories that brought us here.

"How lucky for you then, Ms. River. You get to live the dream for the first time. I doubt we'll get arrested, though. We're miles from civilization, so the sky is the limit. Let's be hedonistic for a night and create a memory we'll never forget!" He pirouettes rather gracefully for a man his size.

"I guess I could have one drink." Teasing him is fun. I'm always acting the square to his circle.

Moonshine is stunned silent before finding his voice to disinvite

Chapter 22

me. "No, no. This is a party for party people. You can't come if you're not going to bring a keg-stand attitude."

"Keg stand? What's that?" Letting him believe I'm ignorant of anything considered edgy by those under twenty-five helps elevate his already high level of cheer.

"All right. You've forced my hand. I will take you, River Jordan, under my wing and teach you everything you need to know. You drink what I give you, smoke what I give you, swallow what I give you."

I smack him hard. "Hey. I've got a boyfriend already."

"You are divine, girlfriend, but you wish! I was talking about pills and not my man-juice."

"Gross!" Always forthright, I love the little shocks he includes in his dialogues.

"Nope. Liquid heaven, but none for you." He wags his finger at me. Then he stops and pulls off his pack. He hands me his sacred kit and tells me to clean up and meet him at the next clearing within the hour.

I look through and find everything I could possibly want to beautify myself. Lucky me, I'm mere feet from a flowing brook.

Ahh, the sheer delight of feeling soap lather between your hands. The bar must contain a conditioner because my skin feels soft and smooth before I use the moisturizer. I know this bottle costs about one hundred dollars, and I relish in every stroke. More of a masculine scent than expected, it dissipates after absorption, leaving me smelling like a clean ocean breeze.

Wanting the feeling of clean to last, I put my pj's on early. I give my dusty trail clothes a good wash and rinse, then clip them on the outside of my pack to dry.

Now that I'm fresh, I'm looking forward to a party. My version, not Moonshine's next-level style.

At least fifty people show up for the festivities: hikers, townies, friends of people on the trail. It's crazy how in just a few short hours, the woods morph from serene to mayhem. Get in line for the rope swing that takes you ten feet out for a thirty-foot drop into a lake that's ninety feet deep. Play volleyball, corn hole, or hide-and-seek; gotta have the kid games. Then, of course, we have Moonshine, the host with the most. He's walking around, a rigged pack slung in front of him like an old-time cigarette girl, peddling everything from Jello shots to chewables to mushrooms, and my choice of the night, lager beer.

"Honestly, Jordan. I had such high expectations," he criticizes me as he hands me the icy brew. Waving his hands over his goodies model style, he upsells the products, "It's all free for the taking. Can I convince you to take one small gummy bear?"

"No."

"One little Jello shot? All cherry." He wiggles his brows, such a salesman.

"Okay. You talked me into it." I have to climb a mountain tomorrow and don't want a hangover hitching a ride, but no one wants a buzzkill at a party. Ever the gracious guest, I make his day. "I'll take two. They're small."

He jumps for joy, clapping his hands. "Keep up the great attitude and come back for more."

As I start to walk off, balancing all three containers, two giggling females approach Moonshine and point at what they want. "Use your words, ladies." I wink at Moonshine, letting him know I'm on to him, and find a spot to sit.

Moonshine makes the young ladies cup their palms to receive a handful of mushrooms each. They begin nibbling right away. It's evident from their expressions they taste disgusting, but they continue to nosh.

No one has fallen for the mushroom gag except this remarkably young-looking group of scruffy townies. They don't know that Moonshine is an expert in all things woodland, including what mushrooms are safe to eat. These won't do a darn thing to their psyche, nor, lucky for them, will they kill them. It's one of his favorite harmless pranks, and it goes off without a hitch, leaving him even more excited than when I accepted the alcohol.

Chapter 22

Though I've eaten my fill, the scent of barbecue still lingers. As one of the older hikers in this group, they only expected me to show up, which is fine with me. They lugged in hibachis, burgers, salad fixings, chips, everything you could want, more than a mile into the woods, along with all the games and adult libations.

Summer is waning, and a definite vibe of "Get it in while you still can" is in the air. We all know, before too long, we'll be freezing our butts off again, wiping our endlessly runny noses in the cold air, and waking up with frost coating the world.

I sit on a rock, still warm from the sun, now setting in the sky, and nurse my beer. It's my favorite time of day; the alcohol adds to my sense of well-being. After ten hours of hiking, with a hearty meal digesting in my belly and hanging out with friends, it doesn't get any better than this.

Until it does, when my phone pings Adam's text tone.

I have some news that I hope will make him happy. Instead of responding in kind, I hit dial.

"Hello, Miss Popular." Ever since I "dumped" him for Kim, he's adopted the moniker.

"Hello, Mr. Grudge." It's our private version of using trail names. Passive-aggressive but playful. "I have something to tell you. Don't take it the wrong way, okay?"

"Okay," he sounds less than committed.

"Kim can only stay one night, which still leaves us open to having a night together." I have my fingers crossed. I know men are as sensitive as women. They just don't show it the same way. "Please say yes."

After a short pause, he says, "Well, gee, I don't know. I mean, we had these plans. Then we didn't. And now you want to throw me half a plan. It's a lot to consider."

I'm not sure if he's serious. I play along in the hopes he's making me work for it to save his pride. "Hmm. Is there anything I can offer to sweeten the deal?" There is no mistaking the innuendo in my voice.

He rewards me with his honey-thick, throaty laugh. "Oh, you can be sure I can come up with lots of ideas. Do you promise to fulfill every last one of them?"

"Yes." Imagining us together has me desperately willing to agree to any of his demands. I just want to make sure they are in the interest of us both.

"Then, my sweet hiker, we have a deal. One night in Massachusetts. Give me the particulars so I can get to planning."

I give him dates, times, and the name of the hotel. "Thank you for being so accommodating, Adam. Kim needs me."

"She's lucky to have you. Jonathan has been causing lots of trouble around here, and I suspect he's just as hard on Kim."

"Are you okay? You sound tired."

"Are you trying to disinvite me again now that you've made big promises?"

"Oh, no. I'm a woman of her word. I'm going to give you all you ask for down to the letter." I hear a deep moan in response.

"You're killing me. I'll admit it's been exhausting, but it's mostly your fault."

"Hey, no need to get nasty about it."

"There are plenty of reasons to get nasty, Jordan." Adam reminds me of our common goal. "I'm glad you were able to fit me in. Seriously. Work has been taking its toll, and missing you has me up all hours trying to exhaust myself with exercise. I can't tell you how much I'm looking forward to our visit."

"Me too. Please take care of yourself, okay?"

"I will, Jordan. You as well."

After saying goodnight, I put the phone in my bag.

Full dark has fallen, someone just turned the music up to the highest decibel, and people are dancing around small campfires like our tribal ancestors. At the swimming hole, clothes have come off for skinny dipping. Removing my own, I head to the rope swing and cut in line. Hoots, hollers, and catcalls abound. I run with the rope and jump, soaring through the air. As my feet slice through the water, the icy cold chill tames the fire Adam started.

23

JORDAN

Kim beats me to the hotel room, where she's already two glasses into a cheap bottle of red wine.

"You came prepared," I quip, noticing three similar ones lined up in front of the TV. "Let me clean up, and I'll join you."

I wash my clothes first, rinsing them multiple times before the water finally runs clean. The volume of dirt that collects on the smallest piece of cloth never ceases to amaze me. Some days, my socks can stand on their own.

I hang everything here and there, knowing the quick-dry fabric will have them ready for packing by morning. Not that I'll be leaving. Adam arrives a short time after Kim departs. I'm thrilled to be able to spend time with both of my friends.

Now it's my turn to shower, and it takes roughly the same amount of suds and rinses to get off the grime. It leaves my skin feeling squeaky clean and somehow not my own. My fingernails undersides are black, so I spend extra time with the washcloth and soap bar before shutting it all down.

Wrapping myself in a towel with another twisted around my hair to sop up the excess water, I head out to the bedroom to fill my glass.

Kim is in a fetal position, crying on the bed. I sit quietly by her side, handing her tissues and rubbing her back.

"I miss Jonathan so much I can hardly breathe. How did you survive your breakup with Brett with such ease?"

My laugh is harsh. "I wouldn't say it was easy, but it was a relief. And it was different with Brett and me; I was happy to see him go. It will get better. You just have to give it time." I refill both glasses when she's ready to sit up and drink.

She takes a long swallow, finishing the contents before holding the glass out for more. "I don't think I can do it. I want him back so bad."

"Maybe we should get some food." I hand her the room service menu, which she tosses to the side.

"I'll have whatever you're having." To slow her drinking pace, I make the call before she continues. "What does it matter? He just thinks I'm a fat cow no matter what I do."

"Does he say that?" I'm trying to focus on supporting her when all I want to do is shake her and say, *Are you kidding me? He is, has always been, and will always be an asshole! After your second date with him, I told you this when he tried to kiss me and push me into your bedroom while you were sleeping on the couch!*

She fluffed it off the following day, saying, "Boys will be boys." I couldn't convince her that this was no schoolboy fantasy, that there was something more aggressive about it, but she wouldn't hear a word of it. Within a handful of dates, she was already planning the engagement party. Almost fifteen years later, she still refuses to see him for who he is.

"Yeah. But Jonathan says he's just kidding."

"You're not fat. You're the same size you were before you had Liam. It's called verbal abuse, Kim."

She waves me off. "No. It's not like that. He feels bad every time he does it and always makes it up to me. That's why he booked us the spa day."

Gee, and that doesn't sound like textbook abuser behavior? I bite my tongue so that the words don't spill out.

"I thought it was because your pipes broke?"

Chapter 23

She's drunk enough to tell me the truth. "That was just a story. Jonathan doesn't like houseguests."

I blurt out, "Jonathan doesn't like me."

She nods, eyes already at half-mast, causing her glass to tilt. I hand her the towel from around my head to wipe up the spill.

"He thinks you're a bad influence." She laughs like she expects me to join her.

"I never understood that."

She sits on the edge of the bed to reach the bottle for another refill. I encourage her to wait for the food, but she insists.

"Remember when we went to Cancún, and you and Ruth left me on the beach?"

"Yeah. I'm still sorry about that."

"S'okay." Her slurring has begun in earnest. "You were never great at math."

Three of us went down for spring break, Kim, Ruth, and me. Once we arrived at the hotel, we found the place swarming with other people our age. One group, in particular, stood out. Five guys, college buddies like us, began talking and flirting with us anytime we left our rooms. They were funny and handsome, and we hit it off from the beginning. We started going everywhere together: snorkeling, fishing, parasailing. Our days ended getting trashed in each other's rooms, at the bar, or on the beach.

One night, we joined a party already in progress on the beach. There were so many people dancing, singing, and up to all kinds of hijinks. None of us were what you would consider shy, and we didn't stay close. I hung out with a few locals to work on my Spanish, Ruth hooked up with a girl from a rival school, and no one knew Kim would end up missing.

We stayed out until three in the morning and called the hotel shuttle service to pick us up. I thought I did the headcount right, but I was as drunk as everyone else.

When we got back to the hotel and realized we were down three people, Kim was one of them. She told us she slept at the beach until five and then began walking. A cab passed by, and she flagged it down.

Kim was back at the hotel and sleeping when we all woke up close to noon.

It's one of the few things I still feel guilty about from my past. Kim could have become a statistic being left alone that way, not knowing anyone.

"On our first wedding anniversary, Jonathan took me out to dinner. Guess who came up to our table?" Kim struggles to remain upright now that she's into her second bottle of wine as she continues to talk.

I shrug. I have no idea where she's going with this.

"Damon." She smacks my side. "Remember Damon? Black hair, seemingly blacker eyes, bulging muscles covered in tattoos?"

"Oh, yeah. Damon was such a funny guy." All of them were. It was a memorable week.

"Well, he brought the story of that night up, and I couldn't let Jonathan know the truth, so I told him it was you."

"What was me?" How is falling asleep on the beach a story you couldn't share with your husband?

She gives me a sly look, putting her finger to her lips, and says, "Shh. Don't tell anyone, 'kay?"

"Okay." I'm not sure I want to hear it either.

"You didn't leave me on the beach. I was hiding. With Damon. And Jeff." She covers her mouth with a feigned look of shock. "We did it for hours."

"Hid?"

She bursts out laughing, wine spewing in my face. "No, silly, we were having sex. Lots and lots of sandy sex." She gets serious again. "But don't tell. Jonathan would think I was a slut."

Kim has hurt me on so many levels. I hardly know where to start. Should I even bother?

With her share, it sounds as though she and Jonathan are perfect for each other without them even realizing it.

So Jonathan thinks I'm the one who is promiscuous instead. Do I care? I mean, I can't stand the guy, and right now, I'm not feeling like the biggest fan of his wife, either.

Chapter 23

A loud knock at the door saves me from tearing into her about the unfairness of her behavior.

I give the delivery gal a big tip and bring the food tray inside. I decide to let the matter go and find it has already taken care of itself. Kim is asleep with her empty glass still clutched in her hand. She probably won't remember the conversation, and I doubt I'm ever going to bring it up. Knowing doesn't change the past.

As I tuck into the two orders of fried chicken, mashed potatoes with gravy, and corn, I ponder on how messed up my friend is. That I will forgive her is inevitable, but will I be able to trust her again? I don't know.

Now *I'm* the one who feels like crying. I shove the feeling down with extra-crispy goodness and more wine.

Kim wakes the following day on a sour note. She's hungover and angry with me for not finding what she did funny.

"We wrote all your term papers that semester, Kim! Ruth almost failed out because she wanted to make it up to you. You should have been the one making it up to us." My idea of never bringing it up didn't happen. The more time went by, the angrier I got. Last night was the worst night's sleep I've had in a bed in a long time.

"We were on vacation! And what did you care? You got better grades than the rest of us without even trying."

"I studied constantly, and that's not the point. You should have told us. We were scared to death when we realized you weren't at the hotel."

She lifts her arms, exasperated. "You were both dead to the world when I got back!"

"We passed out." It sucks to admit the truth when I'm feeling sanctimonious. "The guys brought over a bottle of tequila while we were trying to figure out how to find you. Once we laid down to rest, we were gone. Look, it wasn't a nice thing to do. That's all I'm saying."

She slumps down next to me on the bed. "You're right. I wasn't the most considerate person back then. You always got along with all the guys by just being yourself. I was embarrassed about what I did and made you and Ruth pay for it."

"Kind of like letting Jonathan think it was me."

She takes my hand loosely in hers. "I did. Do you want me to tell him the truth?" She looks scared as hell that I might say yes.

I hope this doesn't mean she'll be getting back together with him, but ultimately, that is her decision to make. "No. Jonathan's opinion of me doesn't matter."

"Is this going to change how you care about me?" She holds up her hands to stop me from answering. "Wait. Before you say anything, maybe this will sway your opinion. Threesomes never work out. Believe me. I convinced myself I enjoyed it, but I didn't. The alcohol buffered everything, giving me the impression it was a good idea.

"I was always seeking attention, and I was willing to take it any way I could get it. In my screwed-up thinking, I believed if one man wanted me, that was great. But two men? That must mean I was something special." She lets out a bitter laugh. "Being used is never special, though. Honestly, they were as messed up as me.

"Damon ended up getting into heroin. He was out celebrating his second sober anniversary when we met up with him. And Jeff." She shakes her head as if to dispel the memory. "He committed suicide a few years after graduation. I never told anyone, but he and I stayed in touch. He had a few run-ins with the law, at least one burglary charge, and couldn't hack the prison flashbacks. I'd lend a kind ear now and again." She clutches my arm and implores me to believe her next statement. "We never had sex again! One time was more than enough for me. But, he continued to relive the horror of his abuse, and even though I encouraged him to get help, he refused. I stopped hearing from him for over a year until I got one last letter out of the blue. It was a suicide note, and I contacted the police in his town. I was two days too late.

"So you see, it was a bad choice, made by three suffering people. We all ended up with very different results. I'm so lucky I straightened up. I could have just as easily ended up like Damon, or worse, Jeff."

Chapter 23

"I wish you hadn't gone through all that alone, Kim. I'm your friend. Plus, I think you're a wonderful woman who has learned her lessons. I'm sorry they had to be so harsh. You're a great mom, and besides the deception, you have been a true friend. You helped me stay sane when Brett and I split, and he kept harassing me so."

"You're the best friend I've ever had, Jordan." She bumps me with her shoulder as I sit, thinking of my past hardships. "What do you say? Do you forgive me?"

"Yes. But lie to me again, and the kid gloves are coming off."

"Deal."

24

ADAM

Trying my best to be stealthy, I key into the room. Jordan assured me Kim left hours ago, and I see no evidence of either woman, save Jordan's signature sprawl of detritus.

Light from the bathroom floods the far end of the space. Leaving my things by the door, I head toward it.

Fully nude, Jordan's body still drips with water from the shower. She's looking down at her phone, brushing her teeth in a distracted fashion.

She looks even fitter than the last time I saw her, more angular, less curvy, but with plenty of woman left for me, not for anybody else. At least, that's my way of thinking.

I slowly take in every line and contour of her body, starting with her delicate ankles. Jordan's wounds have healed completely, leaving the skin taut and smooth from her calf through her hip and across her flat belly. Lingering at her breasts, I find the break in the tan lines alluring. I catch her eyes in the mirror, watching me watch her.

"Hi," she says simply, after rinsing.

"Hi." I watch as an errant water droplet skips down her chest, over the swell of her breast, to land on the edge of her hardened nipple. I cross the gap between us. Her body shudders as I use the tip of my tongue to lick it off, relishing the taste. I thread my fingers through her thick hair and kiss her ready mouth. "You taste so sweet. I've missed that."

"I've missed *you*." She's panting with want already as she unbuttons my shirt, trailing kisses across my chest.

I pull her flush against me, her wet skin dotting my clothes with moisture, reminding me I have too many garments on. I grasp her firm, pliable bum and lift her to sit on the counter.

Way ahead of me, Jordan's pushing my shirt from my shoulders. As it falls to the floor, she begins tugging at the button on my jeans, so I reach down to help. Her fingers dance across my abdomen. One of her hands dips lower and wraps around my erection. I'm already close to the brink and have to stop her.

"I want to take this slow."

"No time for slow, Adam. Time for now."

Somehow she has a condom in her hand; my forest sprite comes ever-prepared. Sheathing me quickly, I can tell that her need is as desperate as mine as I enter her slick warmth.

With one thrust, I'm buried deep, causing her to moan out loud. Her eyes dilate as she demands, "Love me, Adam."

And I do.

JORDAN

"You brought me presents." My voice is thick from our lovemaking. Roses, champagne, and chocolates, he hands me in rapid succession. I tease him, "You sure have the schmaltz down."

Feigning anger, he tries to take my gifts away. "Why, you little ingrate. I can eat all those chocolates by myself."

"Nooo." The box rests on my belly. For every two I eat, I let him have one. I plop another candy into my mouth and kiss him, blending chocolate, caramel, and liqueur. "I'm playing. But, I have had enough sugar for one sitting."

He watches me cover the uneaten portion and place it on the bedside table. "How about I order us some real food?" he asks as he reaches for the phone. "What are you in the mood for?"

"Surprise me."

"You got it, my gorgeous foodie."

After he orders, we snuggle on the bed, while I trace his muscles one by one. "You did work out a lot. It looks like you've been doing one of those infomercial workouts."

"Nope." Adam plays with my hair while he talks, spreading it across his chest. The strawberry scent has me thinking about fresh fruit. "Mostly the running and swimming laps. Some weights."

"You would kick ass on the trail, I bet. Do something constructive with all you've attained. Interested yet?"

"Not in the least."

"Shucks. You can't blame a girl for trying. Come on. We could hike during the day and do this every night. Wouldn't that be fun?"

"Not really," he says.

I sit up and push away. "What? You don't think this is fun?"

He uses a fingertip to trace the outline of my lips before trailing it down to glide along my collarbone. When his hands head further afield to play with my breasts, my skin chills yet somehow feels set on fire. Still not answering my question, he explores my belly button with the same slow, measured pace. Unwilling to allow the giggle out—Ugh! It's so annoying to be ticklish—I bite my inner cheek to help me stay quiet.

As his touch travels further south, he finally answers me. "This is the most fun thing I have ever done in my entire life." Instead of continuing with his hand, he angles his head down and uses his tongue between my legs.

I release any grudge as he brings me to another climax.

Chapter 24

I can hear Adam's heartbeat in my ear as I lay against him, one leg tossed over his thighs. He is everything I remember and more: considerate, sexy, and an expert at thrilling my body.

Adam is pestering me again the way he did the first time he dropped me back on the trail. "Why don't you end your hike now? This mini-break will be our celebration. Come back home with me, and we'll do this."

"Just this?"

"Okay. I'll feed you too. Deal?"

Though part of me would love to agree with his inadequate bargain, my mother didn't raise a quitter. Maine may still be a long way away, but I am not stopping now.

"You're funny, but no, thank you." I'm barely holding on to consciousness, but I want dinner before I sleep. "It's because I smell on the trail, isn't it?"

"It's because camping sucks."

I open my mouth to rebut his silly remark, but loud knocking interrupts my thought process.

Saved by the bell, Adam pulls on his pants to answer the door for room service.

I roll my naked self up in the sheets. It might look like Adam might be hiding a body, but the delivery guy doesn't seem to care.

The door barely closes, and I sit up, fork in hand.

Adam laughs. "You're priceless, Jordan. You know that, right?"

25

JORDAN

I sit at the table, wrapped in a fluffy white bathrobe. "Kim sure picked a great hotel." Adam might have trouble understanding what I just said, considering the size of the bite I took out of my cheeseburger. I followed it with a handful of fries and a gulp of chocolate shake, so thick it's like they didn't bother to add the milk.

"Nice enough to kick us out if you ate like that in the restaurant."

I fling a wrinkly little grape tomato neither of us wanted to eat at Adam, proving his point.

"You eat like a bear in a dumpster."

The observation has me laughing and rolling in the chair, clutching my belly. "No," I struggle to speak through my cheer and my as of yet not swallowed food. "Come on. Maybe a pig at a trough. I'll give you that."

I try to eat one fry at a time, but it's impossible. I'm too hungry, and they are so thin and crisp. The salt alone fulfills a fundamental need as I naturally lack enough sodium chloride. I can feel it plumping my tissues as it balances my fluids.

"I like it; your approach to all things carnal." He toasts me with a glass of champagne. "You don't hold back."

"True. But you keep up the insults, and I might hold something

Chapter 25

back." The warning holds no weight whatsoever. I could no more stay away from Adam than from the trail. It certainly leaves one in a quandary. I remind myself of the quote, "You can have it all, just not all at once." Now I have him, and tomorrow, I'll be hiking once more. It's all good.

Calling my bluff, he picks me up and tosses me onto the bed.

"Oh no, you don't, mister. I know when I've been insulted." I reach for the blankets too late. He shoves them to the foot of the bed and unties my robe.

"New rule." His eyes are dark with lust. His words come out in a low timbre. "No clothes until you leave. I can't have you threatening us in that fashion." He licks my belly button, knowing it tickles.

"Us?" I only have enough brain capacity to use the single-word inquiry as he flips me onto my front, massaging all my aching back muscles.

"That's right. You can't fool me. You want me as much as I want you." His strong hands leave my now loose shoulders. Using his thumbs, he kneads all the muscles marching down my spine.

"Ahh, that feels so good." Onto the divots in my hips, he uses his palms to soothe the tension caused by days spent hiking with a heavy pack weighing me down. "I'm going to fall asleep."

Manipulating my buttocks, giving it more attention than my other muscles, he glides as smooth as silk between my legs, coming to rest inside me. Licking the lobe of my ear, he whispers, "You don't need to stay awake on my account."

I moan as he moves languidly in and out. "Another minute won't kill me."

"No way. I'm taking my sweet time with you."

With slow, rhythmic strokes, Adam's hands trail the curve of my hip to the hollow of my waist. After tracing the line of each rib, his fingertips caress the sides of my breasts feather-soft before moving them beneath me to play with them lovingly. He teases my nipples until they are rigid and wanting more. Instinctively knowing this, he removes himself from inside me, causing me to protest. "Nooo. It's so good."

Ignoring me, he rolls me to my back and slides back into place between my thighs.

"Better?" he asks simultaneously to my "Oh my, yes!"

He cradles me close as his internal strokes begin to increase with my deepening breaths. Kissing me crazy, I urge him with my hips to go faster.

"Uh-uh-uh." He scolds me. "My turn." He tangles his tongue with mine, slow and sensual, like all his other moves. "Just enjoy. We're going to be at it a while."

I moan as he kisses his way down my neck. His thrusts never cease, and I continue my quest for harder, faster, deeper. He forgets himself and gives me just that. "Oh my, yes! Don't stop." I'm so close.

He stops his accelerated pace.

"Nooo!" I call out. This can't be happening.

"You tricked me, Jordan. What am I going to do with you?"

He kisses my answer away. When his hands find my nipples taut and ready, he moves his wet mouth lower, pulling one into the warm recess. He takes his time, laving it with his tongue and teasing it with the light stubble of his beard. He stops only long enough to give ample attention to my other breast.

"You're killing me. Please, Adam."

It takes only one word for him to dash my hopes.

"No. I gave it to you hard and fast the moment I got here." Pulling out, he goes silent to focus on the freckle patterns scattered across my belly, tracing them with a fingertip. "I want you so very much."

When his mouth finds my core, I'm already on fire from his ministrations, and I crest almost immediately. He uses all his tricks to bring me over the top until I'm spent and empty.

But wait! There's more! Adam crawls back up the length of me, pausing at my breasts to kiss each tip sweetly.

Getting settled once again, he kisses the edges of my lips, the lids of my eyes, and asks, "May I finish?"

"Yes." I'm breathless and relaxed to the point of floating, but once he enters me fully, I'm instantly ready for more.

This time he gives me all I desire. Whispering tender words in my

Chapter 25

ear, he quickens the pace as he fills me up only to withdraw almost completely, over and over, until I'm once again standing at the edge of bliss.

I hear him call out my name the exact moment my release bursts through my womb, spreading to consume me.

It takes us a few minutes to gain our bearing and our breath. Adam rolls off me, pulling me close to spoon my body with his.

"You okay?" His breath tickles the moisture on my skin.

"Better than." I snuggle in closer, his arms powerful around me.

※

Awake before Adam, I realize I never brushed my teeth before falling asleep last night. Feeling like someone slipped tiny sweaters over them as I slept, I gently remove Adam's arm from around my waist and head to the bathroom. My body feels well-tended and sore in certain unused places. It's a delicious ache that leaves me wanting more. But first, I must locate coffee. Not in the room, crazy pod coffee, real coffee.

He catches me in the act of dressing and mumbles, "I believe I told you no clothes."

"Your priority. Mine is coffee."

"Approved," he says, grasping my hand, kissing its palm. "Grab me one, would you?"

Adam is in the shower when I return to spread breakfast on the small table. I sit and relish in the hot energy-bearing drink while considering whether or not to remove my clothes. I'm sure what Adam said was in the spirit of the moment, but a woman needs to be sure. The package and the person don't always line up, and I need more proof. Past infidelity leaves its scars.

The shower turns off, but I'm too hungry to care.

The truth strikes me like lightning. Small as it is, I'm making decisions for myself, not for someone else. I can't say I'm not looking forward to our next lovemaking session. Adam is correct about it being the most fun thing ever. But I'm prioritizing my needs right now. Somehow, my coffee tastes even better.

Grabbing a cherry and walnut muffin from the bag, I sit and enjoy my breakfast and personal growth.

"Good morning." He swoops in and kisses my neck. "That was quick."

"They have a real bakery downstairs that serves lunch as well." Always thinking ahead, I noticed they had a Thanksgiving club sandwich with all the trimmings.

Adam sits across from me and picks out the cinnamon caramel muffin.

"I pegged you as a blueberry man."

His eyes crinkle at me over his coffee. "That doesn't sound like much of a man. The blueberry man." He shakes his head. "Almost as bad as the muffin man."

"At least you're not the muffin top man."

"That's thanks to you."

"I'm going to make business cards, I think. It's a unique talent to train people from hundreds of miles away with no interaction. My coaching skills are bordering on magical. Yes, Bordering Magic. That would be a good name for it."

"Your motto could be, "One look at me, and you'll be running for the hills.""

I frown at his joke. "You're lucky I'm hungry, or you'd have a lap full of crumbs."

He pulls me onto said lap in one lickety-split motion. "I'd rather it be full of you." He kisses me, smooth coffee covering his tongue. Delicious. "I meant it in a good way. I had to keep running, or thoughts of you would drive me crazy." His hands begin roaming as he lists my assets.

Of course, my phone picks this moment to start pinging Edge's melody, even though I haven't seen him since he stormed off into the night. Which reminds me, I'm supposed to ask Adam if he knows why.

First things first, I wiggle out of Adam's arms. "I have to take this. It's Edge."

He folds his hands firmly around his coffee cup tight enough to pop the top off and splash the remaining liquid on the floor. I grab him a wet towel from the bathroom and then sit on the bed to read through the thread.

After a few minutes, long enough for me to read it multiple times, Adam breaks the silence. "So, what does he have to say?"

Absorbed in trying to understand what it all meant, I forgot I wasn't alone. I tell Adam, "I don't know. But he says it has to do with you."

26

ADAM

"Edge doesn't give you a reason why?" I ask Jordan the question, knowing how ill-prepared I am for this. Too bad the jig appears to be up, and I don't see a way out.

"Nothing specific. Perhaps you'd like to fill me in." She crosses her arms, shutting herself off to me.

"Not unless he gives us a clue." *Wimp!* The accusation belts out so loud in my head, I'm shocked she can't hear it too. How will I ever explain my side of the story without sounding like a terrible person or the world's worst executive? The intricate details of the injury might be the same, but certainly, the fallout for both of us is worlds apart.

The worst part is that I lied to her. I should have told Jordan who I was that night by the pool, how I knew her friend. Maybe I could have convinced her that I tried to do the right things after the accident. She'll never believe me now if I tell her that my heart was in the right place. I wanted to give us a chance and was afraid to ruin everything with my human frailties.

"He wants to meet me in an hour. What should I tell him?"

I gird myself. This whole situation has only one mature response. I say it knowing this could be the end of everything. "Let Edge know you're with me. If it's okay with him, I'd like to come along."

She types as I speak, thumbs flying. Seconds later, she has his answer. "He says he'd like you to go to hell." Her expression is one of concern with traces of distrust. "But you can come."

I reach out, touching her shoulder. She visibly cringes, jumping up to stand. "We better get ready." Incapable of looking at me, Jordan focuses on tossing our meal's remnants and straightening things that don't need attention. She swipes at her eyes, and I see she's crying.

"Hey." I don't touch her but stand close. "It's going to be okay."

"My gut says you're wrong, Adam."

※

JORDAN

I insisted on bringing my backpack to have options, no matter what happens. I have no idea what we're going to be coming up against as we cross the parking lot to meet with Edge. The French bistro hostess takes us to an outside eating area surrounded by trees and flower-filled containers. The only person in the courtyard is Edge.

He greets me as he always does in front of others, aloof, with a quick tilt of his head. I introduce him to Adam though I recognize it is redundant. They know each other, and I'm the only one who doesn't know how.

Adam pulls out my chair, the metal grating on the concrete. With my instincts for danger cranked up high, my body reacts with a twitch before sitting. Adam takes the chair beside me as he nods in Edge's direction.

Edge speaks first. "What did you tell her?" He's shooting daggers in Adam's direction, while Adam keeps his hands folded in his lap, bearing up under the scrutiny.

I've watched many men back down when confronted with Edge's ire. Maybe there was hope.

"Nothing. This is your story. I'm just a part of it."

Edge turns his attention to me. "Do you know what your sweetie here does for a living?" His words are bitter and barely tempered.

I remember the first night at Adam's place. No doubt, watching paint dry would have been more exciting than listening to another word about board meetings and interoffice fighting.

"Adam works in a business office. That's all I know."

"That's convenient. But, no, he works as a colossal dick, his official title, in my opinion, and is CEO of Advanced Automation. A robotics corporation. *The* robotics corporation that destroyed my life."

My stomach falls to the floor as thick, viscous dread floods my system. I'm going to be sick. I take deep inhales and long exhales, trying to keep the bile down. No dice. I bolt inside the tree line and what's left of my breakfast heaves to the ground. Covering my tracks being so second nature, no one besides the three of us will ever know it happened.

Returning to the table, I take a long drink of water and follow it with a few pieces of mint gum. It's a while before I can find my voice. When I do, I address Adam. "How could you?" A short sentence for what I imagine will be a long answer.

His eyes dart between the two of us before coming to rest on me. I have a hard time looking at him, but I do my best as he begins to explain his version of the events Edge shared with me months ago.

"During the first week in Neil's prototype department, the machine worked better than we expected. We put it through multiple lab tests, and each one went without a hitch. It wasn't until after the accident when we discovered one of the delicate linkages in the robotic arm that held the grasper was off by infinitesimal amounts. Things seemed perfect. We had hit our stride and believed it wouldn't be long before we could finalize the patent and get in on the market.

"But, then, it wasn't perfect. During a tour led by Jonathan." Adam pauses to fill Edge in on who Jonathan is.

"I'm familiar," Edge tells him, disdain dripping from his words.

"Okay, well, he showed some of our largest shareholders around. The evidence suggested that someone tampered with the links on the manipulator. No one should have been allowed to get that close. We have thick, bright yellow lines throughout the lab to indicate where people can stand, but they were ignored. Even so, the rule was, before

Chapter 26

every test, that two engineers had to check each joint and attachment to confirm that nothing was loose. But the engineers who were responsible for the detailed exam the following day never bothered with the checklist. So, the parts didn't connect, the unit malfunctioned, and Neil ended up paying the consequences.

"It was negligence, pure and simple." Adam now looks directly at Edge. "That's why we didn't contest the judgment when you sued the company. Per our law team's advice, Jonathan took the stand first, and we agreed with the terms ordered by the judge. It's just money. I get it. It can never make up for all you've lost, but it's all we had to offer. What more can we do? What can *I* do?"

Edge's face turns the ruby tone of rage. It's obvious he's not agreeing with what Adam is saying.

I place my hand on his forearm and whisper, "Edge, just listen until he's through."

He breathes like a dragon through his nose and nods.

"There hasn't been a day since the accident that Neil hasn't been on my mind. It's incomparably the greatest regret of my life and the reason why I haven't had much of one since. I've existed in a limbo of sorts." Adam's smile is filled with sadness. "When Jordan entered into the picture, it seemed I had permission to start living again." His voice falters as he finishes. "That may no longer be the case."

Hands clenched in fists, so tight the knuckles are white, Neil growls, "You're a goddamn liar!"

My eyes ping pong between both men. Adam looks calm, but waves of hot anger are flooding off of Edge. Hoping it won't come to blows, I interject. "Adam, what you're saying is vastly different from the truth. Barely close to what Edge has told me."

Not finished speaking, Edge asks, "Do you know how much my settlement was?"

"I think so. Ballpark, around fifteen million."

Neil laughs uproariously at the amount. However, the sound has no humor in it. "You seriously believe your own bullshit, don't you? I got raked over the coals in court." He points his finger dangerously close to Adam's eyes. Adam still doesn't flinch. "By your company, by your lawyers. The trial barely lasted a week, but the shit they said." Edge's face drips with sweat. "My fault! They claimed it was my fault!"

I try to hand Edge some water, but he doesn't notice, so I drain the glass.

"I got two hundred and fifty thousand dollars after the medical bills were all paid. Apparently, that is the going rate for castrating a man because some rich asshole was allowed to play with a machine worth millions of dollars like it was a Lego set.

"The doctors told me I'm lucky I can still piss after the reconstructive surgeries. I can tell you I don't feel particularly fucking lucky." He stands and grabs his backpack, leaving a five on the table for his coffee now grown cold. "I have nothing more to say to you. You are the lowest form of life possible. I realize you have no integrity, but if you can pretend to have some for just a moment, then you'll let Jordan go. She doesn't need a monster like you in her life."

Turning to me, he says, "I'll wait at the trailhead for fifteen minutes. Stay with him or meet me there. Your call."

He smacks Adam across the face with his muddy pack as he passes, the move clearly on purpose.

Adam calmly wets his napkin and wipes the skin clean.

27

JORDAN

"How could you?" It's the only question I can seem to manage with my emotions vacillating between anger, hurt, and shame. I'm so mad I found the one man who seemed an actual match, a friend, and a lover. And I'm pissed he hurt my best friend. The pain stems from knowing this will destroy my trust in humanity, particularly men, forever. The shame falls like a heavy blanket, covering me completely. I am still so easily hoodwinked.

Adam reaches for my hand. "Don't touch me!" I seethe. "I don't even know you. You're just like the rest, willing to lie and use anyone as long as your own needs get met. You make me sick."

"Jordan, please, let me explain." Adam turns his chair to face me, his forearms on his thighs to look me in the eyes. My head is down so low I don't know how I'll ever walk with it up again. "That isn't how it happened."

I push back to leave. "I'm not going to sit here and listen to propaganda from you."

"I wouldn't expect you to." He glances down at his watch. The candy watch I gave him to wear is still there, right next to his Rolex. He must have slipped it on after his shower. I clamp my heart down at the tender gesture.

"We have ten more minutes before you have to decide to stay or go. Will you please let me share my side?"

I fold my arms across my chest, a personal hug and a barrier to Adam and his words. "Fine." I'll let him talk, but I doubt it will make a difference.

I've seen the injury. I accidentally stumbled upon Edge bathing in a fast-moving creek. He couldn't hear my footfalls in the underbrush above the din of so many swirling whirlpools and miniature waterfalls. It was shocking. His level of self-acceptance makes him one of my heroes.

"I was horrified by what happened. When the call came in, I rushed first to the factory to talk to witnesses, get a look at the scene where it happened, and personally oversee the robot's dismantling.

"Next, I went to the hospital. No surprise, Neil refused to allow me in. I sent the kinds of things you do when people are hurt or sick: flowers, food, money. I told myself, 'Okay, I'll keep doing this until I hear from his lawyers.' But then, the day after he entered the rehab facility, an enormous package arrived for me at work. He sent everything back. Every card, every rotten container of food, every single dead flower was in that box.

"I understood the message: Neil hated me. He was living a nightmare and needed someone to blame beyond a nameless, faceless stockholder who didn't know any better than to keep their hands to themselves.

"So, I called my lawyers. I wanted them to know whatever Neil wanted, Neil got. We tried to settle out of court, but Neil's lawyer was hell-bent on a payout that was sure to bankrupt the company. We had no choice but to allow a judge to decide the appropriate amount for Neil's injuries. The trial began on a Monday, and I was scheduled to testify on Friday. But, by Thursday, everything was settled. Jonathan and the lawyers worked it all out. I was relieved to get past it all and signed the paperwork where the lawyers earmarked.

"You know, Advanced Automation employs thousands of people all over the world. I hated to think of them losing their jobs. We are accountable to the shareholders and, not for nothing, the robots that passed every test, every time, have saved hundreds of lives in the few short years they have been used in operating rooms. A lot of good has come out of all our hard work.

"I'm not going to let this go. If any of what Neil said is true, I'm going to find out. And then I'm going to fix it."

"You can't fix this, Adam." How can he possibly think this way? It's too much. I can't process any of this. He sounds so measured and true, but something is niggling in the back of my brain. It strikes like a cobra. The night at the pool when I thought everything was changing in my favor. I was way off. "Wait. I told you about him. You didn't mention any of this."

"Jordan, you didn't give names. The man in your story could have been anyone. I didn't want it to be Neil." He runs both hands through his hair so hard he leaves grooves. "And you know what? I took the coward's way out. My gut told me that somehow my past wasn't finished with me. But I wanted you so much. You're everything to me."

Oh, the words. Those last four words. Brett used the same ones in our wedding vows. I'm not going through this again.

"No, Adam. I'm nothing." I grab my backpack and flee.

❧

ADAM

The waitress is back to retrieve the bill. "Your friends sure left in a hurry." She tops off my coffee and asks, "Can I get you anything else, sweetie?"

I don't deserve anyone's kindness, rote as it may be. "No. I'll just finish this and be off." The last thing I need is more caffeine to add to the anxiety storming through me. I'm stalling for time to figure out my next step.

"You've got the place to yourself. Stay as long as you like." She maternally squeezes my shoulder before leaving me to my thoughts.

I look around the space. This is how the end of the road appears, like a verdant garden, only empty. Purple, white, and yellow pansy flowers in ceramic pots sway in the breeze, smiling with their creepy faces. Daisies adorn the center of the bistro tables, while white pebbled paths lead one to further seating, creating a mosaic in the shape of a peace sign. I should see beauty, but all I see is the same dead end. If any of what Neil said is true, I can no longer stand behind my company. I've hurt Jordan more than if I had tried. And of course, the real issue, I may very well have been party to twisting a knife in the back of a man who already grossly suffered at the hands of the organization I helped build from the first computer chip up.

I think of how close we came to not having this rendezvous at all. What if Kim could have stayed? What if I couldn't get a flight out? I would consider how it all came to pass a mistake if we hadn't had such a meaningful time. Every moment is seared in my memory. The feelings we shared and the loving words we spoke in truth will have to get me through the days to come. Will Jordan ever forgive me? It's anyone's guess at this point. What I know is the connection we have to each other is real. Because of this, I will never give up trying to win her back.

⚜

When I return to the hotel room, evidence of Jordan is scant, but I can still pick up her lingering strawberry scent. Deciding to leave the roses for the maid, I dump the rest of the champagne and check the room for anything we may have missed. Spying something by the bedside table, I find the black velvet box I'd tucked into her bouquet of roses. She loved the gift, had cried when I showed it to her. She insisted, come hell or high water, I join the rest of her hike hosts, friends, and family when she peaks Mount Katahdin. Jordan wanted to slip the bracelet on as proof of another "Pinch me. I must be dreaming" moment to remind her it was all true, all 2,190 miles of it.

Here is my motivation. I have to fix this by the time Jordan reaches the summit.

28

JORDAN

*E*dge and I have been making up for all our combined lost time, even while surrounded by bugs determined to slow us down. The mosquitos attack at both dawn and dusk. They hate the blistering noonday heat when black midges and deer flies replace them. The midges buzz lazily in front of my face, waiting for the chance to get sucked up my nose, or better still, for me to take off my sunglasses. Then they try like hell to perch on my lower eyelids so they can suck on the light sheen of fluid that prevents my eyeballs from drying up between blinks. The deer flies are no better, but they are easier to kill. They make a gratifying snapping sound when you crush them just so.

I've sure been in a killing mood since I left Adam at the cafe that terrible day. Many a bug carcass lingers in my wake. Edge doesn't quite know how to handle a silent Jordan. He keeps shooting me side-eye looks and being extra conciliatory about breaks and eating rituals. I have no words to express my disappointment. I was happy, dammit! Why couldn't things have simply continued to be wonderful and breathtaking and…magical, so Adam and I could live happily ever after? Probably because no such thing exists. The storybooks lied, period.

When we put Massachusetts behind us, I thought I'd feel relief. I only felt further away from anything that meant something.

When we exited Vermont, I wished I'd never met Adam. I would have missed the joy of falling in love, but then I wouldn't have this empty hole in the heart feeling, either. They quote Shakespeare, saying, "'tis better to have loved and lost." I say, screw them. They can write for a sappy greeting card company because they're wrong also.

Now that we've entered New Hampshire, I'm exhausted. I'm only two states away from being finished, but the thought of all those peaks has me wondering if I'll have what it takes to get through the final push. Specifically, once I'm beyond the Presidential Range, and I still have to contend with Maine. When I share my thoughts with Edge, he suggests I chill on shooting for thirty-mile days. I tell him to zip it. Movement in my body is one of the few things that stops the chatter in my head.

Looking forward to my last planned zero, I focus on my cousin Connie's family reunion being thrown in my honor. Once I peak Mount Washington, I'll hitch a ride back down for thirty-six hours of family time. I should be thrilled, but I can't shake the feeling that I'm missing an integral member of my tree. Brett never felt like family the way Adam did. He felt like home and vacation mixed with holidays and simple pleasures whenever we were together. What else can compare to that? Who else?

Edge breaks my thought pattern. "You ready to stop for dinner?" It's probably a good thing because tears are prickling the corners of my eyes as I envision the peak of Mount Katahdin without Adam there to celebrate with me.

The sun is beginning to sink in the sky as we start to descend the Moose Mountain summit. The mosquitos are back, but the sunset is too spectacular to miss.

"Sure. Mind if we have a fire?" It keeps the bugs away, plus it mesmerizes me into a zone of no thought.

"I'll get on it. You sling the packs."

We've been doing this for so long it goes fast and smoothly. Edge gathers all the twigs and sticks in a hundred-square-foot radius while I toss the rope over a high, thick branch capable of holding close to sixty pounds. This time I get it on the third try. It's as many as I'm willing to attempt before climbing the tree. It freaks Edge out how I can do it without low-lying branches, a vestige from childhood when I had no friends to spot me. The necessity of pitting survival against harm had me practicing from a very young age.

I hide in the tent to brush my hair and clean my face and body before slipping into my pajamas. Though the days are still hot, the nights have turned chilly again. I wear long johns of a space-age material and wool socks. It's one of the most lavish comforts in life, a cozy pair of pj's.

I'm getting pretty sick of trail food. Every mouthful of granola feels like gravel. Pasta, once the love of my life, is becoming a lesson in banality. Even chocolate has lost its ability to give me a dopamine rush. I'm feeling sad over my meager portion tonight. Two Ramen noodles, three beef jerky's, one mozzarella stick, and a sleeve of crackers. Oh, and a candy bar.

I want a big salad piled high with all the fixings: chicken, cheese, bacon bits, a meatball sub, and an ice cream cake, all drizzled with a creamy dressing of any flavor. (Strange and random cravings are a common side effect of my unique lifestyle.) My belly rumbles over my fantasy as I tuck into reality.

"You want the rest of this?" Edge offers me the remains of his instant potatoes mixed with salami, sharp cheddar, granola, and raisins. Weird, but it works.

"Duh," is my only response as I reach for the bowl.

"You know, maybe Adam wasn't lying. I mean, yeah, he's the boss and should know what happened to me that week, but maybe he didn't."

"Maybe I don't want to talk about it," I tell him around a mouthful of food.

"Maybe I do."

I harumph exaggeratedly. "You never want to talk."

"Because you always fill the space with chatter. It's been hell with you all gloomy and morose. Honestly, it sucks. Give him a call. Hear him out." He tries to hand me his phone. For some reason, even though it's a generation behind mine, it always gets better reception.

I ignore the gesture. "What are you even saying? You, of all people, should understand what I'm going through. Adam is not a guy you want to get fucked by."

Silence ensues, and I concentrate on finishing the food instead of weakening to the tears. Being strong will get me through it all, the break-up, the journey. Hell, life. There is no space for sissy attitudes.

"You seemed to be enjoying it," he says when my guard is down.

His attempt at humor sends me over the top. "Ah, for fuck's sake! Why are you torturing me over this?" I gather our dirty stuff and storm off down the path to clean up everything to avoid attracting critters or bears to where we'll be sleeping. The distance helps me get a hold of myself again. He better not pull this crap when we're in bed. I only set up one tent, and I'm not in the mood to talk. A good night's sleep and I'll be as right as rain.

I leave our now clean stuff by a tree and toss my paper trash into the fire. It's fully dark, and we watch the flames dance in the light breeze. Edge pulls me close, wrapping us both in one of the sleeping bags. The ambient temperature is already a good twenty degrees colder than today's high.

"I won't belabor the point. I just want to have my say. Wendy's perspective makes sense: If you didn't know me, you wouldn't know my side of the story. You'd only know Adam's. Maybe that's enough. Think about it."

I have no energy left to argue, so I tell him, "Fine," but don't mean it.

29

JORDAN

*E*dge has left me again for a rendezvous with Wendy, coupled with a recheck of his sprained ankle, and I prefer the alone time. Without him here to pressure me, I walk with my phone tucked deep in my pack and check it only when I need to. It's nice not dealing with Edge's knowing look every time it pings, as invariably, it's Adam. He leaves voicemails and texts saying he's sorry. I know he is. So am I, only for different reasons. I'm sure he wishes that I never found out. I'm bitter about falling in love.

I try talking to my mom, but heaven must be having a connection problem today. I don't get the usual response of hearing her loving voice in my head, feeling her warm presence by my side. It appears I am totally and utterly alone.

Brett has gone M.I.A. Rumor has it that he packed all his belongings from Stacey's place and began driving. My ex always wanted to travel across America. I hope he can find some peace and self-awareness, but I'm not optimistic. If he can leave me alone the rest of my days, that would suffice.

Kim sent a text to let me know she and Jonathan are going to start counseling. I will be affected by the decision, yet have no say. I suppose therapy is always a good idea, no matter which direction it turns.

Jonathan got in touch with me as well. Out of the blue, he left a voice message, telling me if I continue to bad-mouth him in any way, he would make my life a living hell. Having no idea what he was talking about, I let it bounce around in my head for a few days before replying.

I suppose he thought he would put the fear of God in me or something. Not a chance, pal. My life feels rather hellish already, and it hasn't broken me yet. Some arrogant, developmentally arrested adult certainly isn't going to be the one to make it happen.

I left a message, letting him know he had best leave me alone as the police already had a copy of his threat. If anything happens to me, it will be his doorstep they land on first. He's such a twit.

This shedding of the old me was something I was looking forward to when I began. I had no idea the form it would take with the changes being so deeply painful. Somehow, I believed with some distance that I could put the hurt behind me from my marriage, my stepsister, and even my childhood. But it follows you. And I added to the burden by getting close to another flawed human.

I'm not perfect. I have bad qualities, too, but lying has never been one of them. It cuts like a knife to realize that I have invited so many people into my life who don't share the same values. I can't imagine the energy it takes to lie. In that regard, I should be grateful, but today, hostility reigns.

Amid my mental wanderings, I come upon an oasis of water where small brooks have created miniature waterfalls, cascading into a deep, narrow pool. The water is as transparent as glass, yet I can't see the bottom. A test with my fingers lets me know the temperature is refreshingly cold. I'm sold. I shed myself of everything unnecessary, including my intrusive thoughts, and ease in feet first. I cling tightly to the sides, but with the moss, it's no use. I let the water pull me under and bob me back up again. I tend to float with ease and today is no exception.

Brett's mother, Diane, once told me, with all the sweetness of a

Chapter 29

venomous snake, that she used to sink in water until her bones got thin and brittle, and her body mass became softer and less supple. Ah, no, I do not miss the queen of the underhanded insult.

Anyway, I know I'm lots more muscle than she ever was and even more than when I began. Why I float is a magical gift, and that wicked witch can have her snark, her jerk of a son, and her bad attitude.

Unfortunately for Diane, she'll never have her china set. I did sell it. I remember when the woman bartering at the yard sale offered fifty dollars. I insisted it was worth twenty-five and let her walk away with a steal of a deal. *Hm. I guess I do lie. Interesting.*

Oh, well. Back to this moment, and it's glorious. The water is frigid and refreshing against my sweat-soaked skin and overworked muscles; I float for quite some time. Enough so my fingertips shrivel, and the shakes overtake me. A heavy rushing sounds through the bushes just as I'm about to climb out and dry off. *Oh, crap! Bear!* I dunk until only my eyes are showing.

Lucky me, I'm way off. The color is right, black as midnight. The Labrador dog is muddy, slobbery, and thrilled to see another being. With a flying leap, he's in the water, almost drowning me in his zeal to lick my face dry.

"Bear!" A woman commands the dog in a deep voice, "Back off."

I was right in a small way.

Immediately, he swims away from me and begins to do circular laps. It's the only way in the limited space.

"I'm sorry about that," the woman tells me, reaching down to help me out. She wears rings on every finger, including her thumbs, and sports numerous metal bracelets on her wrists. Colorful beaded necklaces surround her neck, draping low enough to graze the top of my head. With her long gray hair hanging free around her and eyes so pale blue as to almost match, she looks like a mountain lady turned feral.

I refuse her help politely in favor of swimming with Bear. It's been a while since I've had playful energy around me. I catch up and match my strokes with his. He's a splashy swimmer, so I give him space to avoid getting the water in my mouth. We get switched around, and he's coming toward me, paws furiously beating the water. I take another dunk, surprising him when I reappear behind him.

He allows me to swim under and around him and quickly learns my pattern. Coming to expect it, he even joins in a time or two by dunking his head and changing direction.

In case it's not obvious, I finally stop for a moment to tell her, "Not a problem. I was expecting a real bear by the sound of him, so this is a pleasant surprise." I dunk to slick back my hair, mussed from our play. "He's handsome. How old?"

"Six years in November, though he thinks he's perpetually six months. He loves people even more than he loves hiking."

I notice she's wearing a light day pack. "You live nearby?"

"Yep. You a thru-hiker?" She looks at my beat-up bag sitting by the trail. My cell phone is buzzing again from the inside.

"Yes. I'm Jordan."

"Margaret. You don't mind us joining you?" She shrugs. "I do remember the manners my mother taught me, even if it's a little late to be asking."

"Meeting new people is always welcome. I should probably dry off anyway." I heave myself out, grabbing a bandana to help wipe off the excess water.

Bear keeps up his exercise regimen, taking in big gulps of water to stay hydrated as he motors along.

Margaret takes a seat on a dry rock. Unzipping and removing the bottom parts of her pants, she dunks her legs into the pool. I own the exact pair, but I sent my lower halves back to my cousin to save pack weight. The daytime temperature should be warm enough for me to get away with shorts for another month. I'll take the rest of the pants with me when I leave Connie's house after the reunion.

"I don't want to pry, but are you going to answer that?"

My phone continues to buzz. Adam is nothing if not persistent.

"No. Is it bothering you?"

She shakes her head. "Doesn't it bother you?"

"No." I give her the short version. I'm used to the buzzing. The sound *is* unpleasant, and like with the bugs that follow me every-

Chapter 29

where, I've learned to ignore it. It's the person texting who has me bothered.

We speak of mundane things. Margaret is a writer for a food magazine, and I beg her to tell me her favorite recipes. She fills my head with all sorts of delightful, decadent treats that I will be availing myself of at the first opportunity.

"Hold on. I've got to get that one written down." To find a recipe with meat, cheese, and pasta that I haven't tried is a keeper. I grab my phone and open up my notes. Of course, it starts buzzing wildly. I can see it's from Adam as his message dances like a ticker tape across my screen. Ignoring it, I prompt her to continue. "Okay. Go ahead."

She says nothing. I look up to find her watching me.

"What?"

"You have a very expressive face. Care to share?"

Margaret has a kind and open face, much like my mom's, so I sit beside her, dunk my legs back in the water, and spill everything: Brett and Stacy, Kim and Jonathan, and finally, my real issue: Adam.

"Sounds like you got more of an adventure than you were looking for."

I touch the tip of my nose with my finger. "You said it exactly right. I expected to get lighter and more carefree as the months went by. The opposite has been true. I was excited about leaving my past behind to find a new me waiting at the finish. Now I feel burdened and overwhelmed like I'm losing one thing after another. And not just the things I wanted to, either. I like Adam. I thought he was different. I'm tired of thinking wrong."

"You're not wrong. People are flawed, all of us. I cheated on my first husband, and my second husband cheated on me. Is it karma? God punishing us? I don't know. But I know that making mistakes is part of the human condition. We make the best choices we can at the moment based on the information we have. Retrospect might be twenty-twenty, but it can also be a punishment. You can't know what you don't know. You did your best; they all did their best. So now, what are you, never mind them, going to do about it?"

Margaret stands to call Bear back to her. He leaps out as though from a platform, coming to land two feet beyond us. He sits patiently, panting while she dries him thoroughly.

"The hell if I know." My phone buzzes again.

"I don't know you, Jordan, but I'm pretty good at reading people. When I look at you, I see sadness, along with all those other things you mentioned. Underpinning it all, though, is hope. Maybe you should explore that adventure as well."

I watch her dig into her pack to remove an apple, plum, and sandwich. Instead of eating it herself, she hands me the jumble. My mouth is watering already for the fresh fruit and bologna with cheese on white bread. Has there ever been a meal so tantalizing? Trail magic this perfectly made-to-order?

"We have to go. You need this more than I do. Take good care, my friend. Remember: If you expect perfection from people, they will let you down over and over again. Not in all cases and not for all people, but allow some wiggle room and space for forgiveness whenever possible. You may be pleasantly surprised." Allowing me a final moment with Bear, she heels him up, and they head off.

"Thank you," I call out before they disappear entirely.

"You're welcome," she says before adding, "Answer your goddamn phone! You're scaring off the wildlife."

30

ADAM

Feeling like a stalker or psychopath, I hit send on my most recent text. Jordan can't keep up the silent treatment forever. Or so I hope. I worry about her terribly when I can't reach her. Something in my gut says Jordan will leave me, which is crazy. I already pushed her away with my lack of transparency. If I could just make her see my heart, I think she would forgive me. Yup. Stalker psychobabble for sure.

Maybe I'll wait a day or two before trying again. I held out the hope that a deluge of messages would have her responding, even in anger, which I would accept with open arms. If I can get the lines of communication open, I think I have a chance of winning her back.

Her blog is on fire again. This time because of pictures posted by her buddy Moonshine. He blacked out the naughty bits, but it is Jordan in the buff on a rope swing. She looks remarkably Jane-like. The photo's feedback is a tad excessive, making me want to invent an internet eraser. I'm not happy about it, but I'm not surprised that people feel compelled to chime in.

I don't even have time for this, but thoughts of her consume me. Not merely her naked internet pic or visions of the times I've held her close, but her humor, her radiant smile, and the all-in way she has of living her life. I miss every bit of her.

I focus on the task at hand and put the phone in my drawer to open Jonathan's computer. It's a viper's nest in here. I've found things from videos of him with women who aren't his wife to pictures of him golfing with the competition's CEO. Jonathan has been playing both sides of the field in his marriage and with the company. He owns stock in two other robotics corporations and is dating no fewer than three different women. In effect, he's cheating with the women he is cheating on.

What I haven't found is anything about Neil. Not a note, a stray thought, or any official records from that period. The lack of documentation is what has me curious. Even if my hunch is wrong, I should be able to find something. Jonathan was the one to testify under oath, and then it was his job to forward the settlement. So why is nothing here? Even I have miscellaneous files from the initial investigation on my home computer. I never asked for the rest because it appeared to go so smoothly. Neil brought the company to trial, the judge came up with an amount, and Advanced Automation paid their debt. Done. Except, not so, as I'm sitting here six years after the fact, trying to put the missing pieces together.

I keep looking for another hour before deciding enough is enough. I'll end up falling asleep at my desk or the wheel if I don't go home soon. Before leaving, I head down to Jonathan's office. The board wants to fill the position by summer's end, but I'm dragging my feet looking at the stack of résumés. I'm not sure that they won't be filling my post too. Everything is so up in the air right now.

I've searched in here before, and it appears nothing has changed. Jonathan left a photo of Kim and Liam sitting on the desk next to his nameplate. I've spoken with Kim a time or two but never bring up the picture. It seems telling, but what do I know about relationships? I had a great one starting and then blew it, trying selfishly to cover my own ass.

I sit in the leather chair and put my feet up in the same position Jonathan would take to look nonchalantly important. He said it

Chapter 30

impressed the underlings. I told him it made him look like a jerk, but he wouldn't take my advice about sitting tall like a big boss.

The view is unremarkable: buildings, windows, patches of sky. Getting lost in thought about Jordan again, I remember leaving my phone in my desk drawer. As I swing my legs down, the chair does a one-eighty, facing me toward a wall of bookshelves. Most of his books are still here, scattered randomly about on the shelves. I lean forward when I notice something reflecting the recessed lights overhead. Pushing aside a thick tome, I spy an open flash drive.

I boot up the laptop one last time and find gold. Pages of court documents. Interviews with people from the lab, the stockholders who were on the tour that fateful day, doctors, nurses, and occupational therapists. I can tell by just skimming the first few pages that the trial was not nearly as cut and dry as Jonathan and the law team led me to believe. All the proof that Neil was telling the truth is within this tiny USB. Jonathan lied and covered up the entire thing. And me, the biggest fool of all, I let him. It's going to take me days to sort through it all, not only the files, but how I could have been so blind. I shut everything down, taking extra care with the evidence, and stop back at my office for my phone.

A call came in while I stepped away, and of course, it was Jordan. I sent her no less than twenty texts and left ten voicemails today, which is how it goes. One moment's inattention and your whole life can change. *For better or worse this time?* I hit the message key, unsure. All I hear is one intake of breath and a click. She didn't say anything. Throwing it down, I pick it right back up and hit redial. Maybe, just maybe, she'll answer.

She doesn't. It goes straight to her enthusiastic greeting, and like a desperate, drowning man, I only have one word left to say. Not help, but "please." I just begged a woman for the first time in my life. I'm not sure it will be the last.

JORDAN

I feel stupid for trying to call Adam back. Kicking myself as I walk the rest of my eighteen-mile day, I decide to drown myself in a nip of brandy, compliments of Moonshine and his impromptu party. I nipped (Ha!) a few just in case I found myself in a pinch, in need of some liquid courage. It's probably not a healthy long-term solution, so I'll leave the behavior on the trail when I go.

As I crack open my second bottle, I decide to read what Adam wrote and listen to what he said in the order it all came. It's just as likely he decided to pull the plug on the whole thing anyway. Maybe he's joined the ranks of so many other men hoping for my downfall. Why chase someone like me down?

With that one question and the few tears creeping down my cheeks, I can tell I'm in the throes of a classic pity party, and I don't care. I feel bad for me, even if nobody else does. I ponder the imponderable. *If a hiker cries herself to sleep in the woods, does it make a sound?*

My pace slows as I read his texts after turning on my headlamp. Each one is sweeter than the last. He starts the thread by asking me to get in touch, progressing to how sorry he is. Then he tells me how he's working diligently to get to the bottom of things, his goal to fix all that has been broken. His voicemails are all about being concerned. He wants to know if I'm choosing to ignore him or something terrible has happened. I remember what a worry-wort he can be. His later texts read like poems with no signs of plagiarism. All his words are authentically his. He tells me how much he misses my lovely voice, beautiful face, and sense of humor. He romantically shares how he dreams of my body joining with his own. His last text and final voicemail hit me the hardest. The text simply states: *I love you.*

Adam speaks into the phone, pleading, "Please."

I'm undone. I polish off the second bottle, quickly followed by the third. Although I may regret this in the morning, I text Adam back, then shut my phone off completely.

31

JORDAN

I wake with a crashing headache and what feels like a mitten in my mouth. It's just dehydration, so I slug down some water before unzipping myself from the tent for my morning ablutions. I start brewing coffee straightaway and hop back inside to snuggle up. It's cold as hell out there this morning. Not quite frost, but a chilling mist hangs low over everything. The heavy wetness forces the cooler temperatures straight into my bones.

When the coffee's ready, I warm my hands with the steaming mug before turning on my phone to map out the day. I like to know where the water is, what the weather will be, and set a goal for how far I think I can get.

Completely forgetting that I texted Adam back in my alcohol haze, the message ping sounds immediately and again three times. Not looking at the thread didn't help me gain peace of mind yesterday, so I choose the opposite tack today and read it in its entirety.

I'm going to keep trying. Along with a heart emoji, that is all Adam writes.

The other ping, it turns out, is from Connie. She briefly fills me in on the details of my arrival. No rest for the weary; I still look forward to seeing all my long-lost relatives.

What a relief. I find nothing to be afraid of here and determine the texts are a good indicator of the kind of day I'll have. Just as quickly, I recognize I'm giving too much power to the messages and the messengers. I endeavor to enjoy my time on the trail regardless and continue focusing on my experience and choices.

I return Connie's text first, letting her know how excited I am. I don't share that I'm also nervous. I could ruin the whole thing and make everyone regret they ran into me again with my bad attitude. I'll fake it if the lousy humor holds.

How will it feel leaving them as I head out on the final lonely stretch? They may be the last friendly faces I see for a long time. I'll have to take lots of pictures to see me through.

I don't know who I'll be when I reach the end or where to go after. I'm technically homeless, even if I carry all my basic needs on my back.

I want to text Adam back and tell him all is forgiven, how we should run off somewhere together to live happily ever after. But life doesn't work that way. Edge is pushing me to reconsider, Margaret seems all gung-ho about forgiveness, and Adam promises me everything but the moon.

So it all comes back to me, one lone soul on a crazy long journey without enough information to make a sound decision. My shoulders slump. I feel more lost than ever. Perhaps being with my family for a short time will help.

I can't stop Adam from trying any more than I can promise he'll be successful, so my reply is simple.

Focusing on my oatmeal and raisins, I work on creating a healthy mindset for the hike. I'll be peaking more than one mountaintop today. The promise of stunning vistas has me excited to begin once again. By early afternoon, I should be within a hitchhiker's distance of the town square and plan to update my blog before heading back out long enough to find a spot to sleep again.

Chapter 31

I'm going to kill Moonshine. Or at least steal his cosmetics kit. That's what I'll do. I'm going to follow all his shelter log correspondence, the attention-getter never misses writing in any notebook along the way, and hunt him until I find him. I'll pounce unawares and get his prize possession. It will be the one thing that will be sure to put this feeling of hell dread resting in my belly like an anvil into his own.

Everyone I know, those I like and those I don't, follows my blog, including my ex-mother-in-law, stepsister, and Brett. It's gross to think all those people have seen me naked, even if I spent six years sleeping with one of them.

Adam. He must have seen the picture. I scroll down the comment section to see if he posted anything. His communications have been nothing but loving and supportive, but if Adam has seen the picture, that could change. He's a tad conservative, so I don't know how he'll react.

I search through the hundreds of posts as quickly as I can. Time is passing by, and I need to find my campsite. I'm tired today and look forward to my nightly ritual.

Adam was one of the first to react, leaving his comment almost at the end. *"You're beautiful, MY woodland woman. Stay safe. P.S. Moonshine, you and I need to chat."*

I find myself quite liking his message. Somewhat proprietary, yet supportive and loving like every other encounter we have had. I'm missing him terribly. He was so kind when I was sick and was exceptionally gracious as my host. And his lovemaking. He made me feel like the center of his world as if nothing else in life could come close.

I want to feel that way again. I crave lying in Adam's arms while trusting him implicitly once more.

Now that I know my heart's desire, how do I go about getting it? A million-dollar question, the only way I'll discover the answer is to get back on the trail. Let the woods weave its magical spell, pour out that potent elixir of omniscience.

I get a ride almost immediately. You can tell this guy helps out us thru-hikers often when he asks me to sit in the truck bed with my stinky pack—his words. It's a brand new truck, so I'm not insulted.

Once my shoes hit the dirt again, I implore the universe to give me the answers I seek, the peace of mind I need—and that the cosmetic bag owned by my wicked friend is easy to find.

❧

I'm surprised to find Moonshine rather quickly. The shelter is so full that latecomers surround the perimeter with their tents. But I am not here to set up camp on my mission of revenge.

I locate Moonshine's tent with ease. It stands out with its bedazzled tent poles and fuzzy dice fobs hanging on the zippers. Knowing what his backpack looks like, I head to a copse of trees. Using my headlight on its lowest setting, I find it dangling from an old oak. Luck must be on my side as his bag is the one closest to the trunk. I don't want to waste a lot of time stringing it back up, plus the noise factor would most likely get me caught, so I scamper up the tree like a squirrel. I feel around the outside of the pack but discover only a few granola bars, gum, and a water bottle. I silently unzip the top one tooth at a time. Justice is mine! Tucking it into my shirt, I head back to solid ground.

Should I leave a ransom note? Yes. Like the Grinch on Christmas Eve, I tiptoe into the shelter and grab the notebook and pen. Knowing my picture has already been shared multiple times, the horse is out of the barn. I would like to have them all deleted, but that is never going to happen. As a general rule, what goes on the internet, stays on the internet. It's an unfortunate reality.

So what do I want? Food, of course.

Dear Moonshine,
If you hope to find your cosmetics bag
intact, you had best leave one meat-filled
sub, along with a large, fresh salad with
creamy Caesar dressing at the third
shelter from this one within the next
twenty-four hours. And cake. A big ol'

Chapter 31

slice of chocolate cake.
No exceptions.

I draw a primitive picture of a river, my staple signature.

Sneaking out as quietly as I came in, I look forward to tomorrow for the first time in a while. I'll be luxuriating in the best skincare money can buy and then eating the meal I've been craving to my marrow. It almost makes being exploited on the internet worth it.

Actually, no, it doesn't, but it's a start.

૬ә

To this day, tree climbing gets my blood pumping, meaning I wouldn't be sleeping anytime soon. I grab the quickest meal I can eat while walking and decide to night hike. It's better this way as I need to keep some distance between me and the other campers. Someone might wake in the night and notice things aren't exactly as they left them.

I may have taken a few minutes to tie some shoelaces together, tossing them up to wrap around a different branch, the teeniest bit higher than the packs—give or take ten feet—on the tree. I probably took some candy out of a bag or two. (Three.) And I definitely moved the propane stoves that were waiting, ready for an early morning coffee or breakfast prep. They'll find them, eventually.

It's no less than what they would have done to me. I've had my shoes go missing, forcing me to walk a mile wearing only the three pairs of socks I carry, the wool ones still soaking wet from the wash and rinse the night before. Someone took my sports bra and flung it on top of the shelter. If I hadn't glanced over when I scrambled up to grab my hanging pack, I would have ended up braless for two days. Not a comfortable thought.

The worst, by far, was when someone stole my good luck charm. It was a plastic bit of nothing in the shape of a shamrock, but it meant something to me. My mom found it one day on the street while we were walking to the movies. We never had a car, so it was either public transportation or our feet. The cinema was close enough to save our bus tokens, and I loved the one-on-one time. My mother would tell me stories, some real, others imagined.

On this particular day, she told me a made-up story of "The Leprechaun, the Rainbow, and the Ant." I don't remember all of it, but the leprechaun was not your happy-go-lucky cereal box kind of leprechaun. No, he was angry and highly protective of his rainbow. He was going to find the pot of gold, and nobody else was going to get close enough to try. He dug and dug and dug, going entire weeks without sleeping, getting angrier all the while. He searched until, one warm day, just after a downpour, he rustled up an ant colony. As he smashed the shovel on them, killing the bugs by the hundreds with each swing, one small soldier got past him. He walked with absolute determination up the side of the rainbow, over great heights as it peaked, and bravely walked down the opposite side, only to find himself deep within a pot of gold doubloons.

To this day, the leprechaun is still digging and obsessing over ants, while the one brave little bug that forged ahead is living in the lap of luxury.

I think her point was to be laser-focused on what you want, not willy-nilly shooting from the hip.

Anyway, just as we arrived at the ticket counter, she looked down and found a green plastic coin in the shape of a four-leaf clover.

"What are the odds?" she asked, then handed it to me. "For good luck. And remember: Luck is made, not bestowed."

I didn't fully understand what she meant back then, but I think I do now.

32

ADAM

Trying to clear out the cobwebs after another night of scant sleep, tossing and turning as I think of Jordan and how to win her back, I head out on yet another run. After waving to my neighbor out watering his lawn before the sun rises, I turn onto the main drag, where the flat pavement has no hidden blind spots. It's quiet at this time of day, but I still run against the traffic. It will take a while for the blood flow to wake me up enough to be aware of more than my pace. I eschew coffee on these early runs, so I don't even have caffeine in my system to help. Some would call me a masochist.

All I know is I physically miss Jordan. Not sexually, but on a cellular level. Okay, some of it may be sexual. I have to admit that she still has me running as much as the massive work stress. Without the exercise, I wouldn't sleep a wink with thoughts of her tantalizing me every time I close my eyes. I follow her blog like a madman. Hell, I've taken to following the blogs of any hikers mentioning her in even the most tangential way. Especially that Moonshine guy. He's as funny as hell, no doubt, but I hope he has taken my words to heart—no more nudes of my lady.

I found a flood of information on the flash drive Jonathan had hidden in his office. It goes deeper than I expected, but, thankfully, not so much that I need to shutter the whole business.

Jonathan took the stand and lied, and the company's lawyers encouraged him. They'll face their day in court; I'll make sure of it. Getting the judge to deem Neil partially responsible for the mishap and order a measly settlement may not be against the law, but pocketing the over ten million dollars left unaccounted for, that's textbook embezzlement and illegal as hell.

I trusted Jonathan because he was a friend long after the friendship had ended. That he could abuse another person so wholly tells me he's a sociopath. He has zero compassion for others and no ability to feel guilt.

I worry over every detail, afraid I might miss something. It's clear that I have already missed more than anyone who calls himself the boss should. Redeeming myself is the single most important mission in my life. If I can do that, I can get the girl. I have to believe this to be true because I don't see any purpose otherwise.

Redemption begins with a choice. Then it's time for action. Therefore, I've decided to resign as CEO of Advanced Automation. I can feel in my gut that this is the right time to move on. It's never been wrong before, and I have no reason to think my instincts are going to fail me now.

Still, I have a lot to do before leaving. I need to make sense of all the information I've found and share it with anyone affected by the fallout. More people will lose their jobs, while others will receive promotions. And, of course, there will likely be ramifications I can't project. To say an unsettled period is on the horizon is an understatement. I'll stay as a consultant until things find their equilibrium, as I still believe in the industry's mission, just not in my ability to keep it growing in the best direction.

I'll need to sell off all my stocks. Once the shares are liquid, I can start plan B. Soon after that, it will be time to tender my resignation. I debate the pros and cons of finding my replacement, but leaving it to the board is smarter. They will have to deal with the choice long-term.

Chapter 32

With too much on my mind, on top of losing Jordan, I realize I need help.

Figuring out my plans and getting them both accomplished with the least amount of strife is a job for Clint. Beyond being a great lawyer, he's an excellent sounding board. He also happens to be an insomniac, so I'm confident he'll take my call.

Slowing my pace to a speakable jog, I greet him when he answers after the first ring. "Hey, Clint. Pardon the heavy breathing. I'm trying to multitask by exercising and deliberating."

"Good morning, Adam. Sounds like my version of a fun time."

"You make it look easier than it is. Do you have time to let me bounce a few things off of you?"

"It'll cost ya." He uses his favorite joke. My checkbook is painfully familiar with his hourly rate.

I tell him what I've been thinking, and he shows me the problems and the holes within. My plan has many, but, hearteningly, none are insurmountable.

"Okay, Clint. We'll do it your way. You agree it makes sense to sell first?"

"Well, it sounds like more is at stake as far as that goes. The market is high. We'll get you a great price. It may take some doing, but it will get done in the time frame you gave me. Are you sure this is what you want? I mean, we're talking an awful lot of money here."

"I know, but I have more." It will put the kibosh on a retirement plan or two, but it won't leave me anywhere near broke. "I'm one hundred percent sure." There is only one thing I want more, and she is not a thing.

"Okay. I'll get my team to start working on it. You focus on the other stuff. Don't let your lawyers at Advanced Automation get involved. At least one of them is culpable too. They'll be going to prison right alongside Jonathan. It's enough for now. Beyond that, I may have to start my own exercising-while-deliberating regimen to come up with more."

I give him a laugh. "Thanks, Clint. I'd say I owe you, but—"

"You're already paying through the nose." He finishes my choice phrase for me.

· · ·

My phone pings as I walk in the front door. Jordan returned a text. Saints be praised! Before I celebrate or crash, depending on her reply, I turn on the coffee maker. Reading the thread through is too fast and such a letdown.

Okay. All she gave me was okay. I poured my heart and soul out and got one word.

I fill a coffee cup and sit by the pool. Instead of seeing the automatic vacuum, I conjure up the memory of us on the stairs, loving each other. Jordan's dark hair shining in the morning sun. Her back is silky smooth, pinching in tightly at her narrow waist. Once I hit the vision of her hips curving generously in my hands, I shake my head to remove the flashback and slug my drink. Still hot as hell, it burns as it goes down. I welcome the pain. I need to focus.

"Okay" is okay with me. It's not a no, and it's not an "F" off. I can work with this.

· · ·

Jordan

"Moonshine!" My voice reverberates in the mountains surrounding us, causing him to jump the slightest bit. Knowing I have the upper hand, I ask, "Do you have the goods?"

"Maybe, Jordan." He curtsies and covers the giggles as he looks to the Adonis standing next to him. Where does he find these guys? Each one is more attractive than the last, and they are always willing to do Moonshine's bidding. The man holds a paper bag large enough to contain my particular food order. I'm salivating but unwilling to let Moonshine off the hook just yet.

Chapter 32

I pull out the cosmetics bag and hold it up for all to see. Everyone is rapt with attention.

Moonshine stands outside the shelter at one end of the wooden platform, me at the other. Besides Adonis and us, River Rock, Katydid, and Whirlpool watch, lined up on the wooden shelter floor, feet hanging toward the ground. They have no idea what this is all about, but it will be worth watching because they are familiar with Moonshine.

"You don't want to mess with me, Moonshine. I'm going to ask you one more time: Do. You. Have. The. Goods?" From my pocket, I pull out a Swiss army knife.

Everyone, including those sitting in the cheap seats, lets out a loud gasp. They all know what this bag means to Moonshine, as well as they understand what I'm threatening.

"Give me what I demanded, and we all walk away happy. Deceive me, and the bag gets it." I shove the sharp end of the mini-blade into the fob and begin to open the zipper slowly to bring the image of me slicing through the soft leather to life.

"You wouldn't dare." He stands as tall as possible with his hands on his hips. Nose in the air, he has the audacity to look down at me.

"You think so?" I make three slashes against the fabric, deep enough to show I mean business, but not sufficient to cause damage. Yet.

"Just calm down, okay?" He holds his hands up in supplication and whispers to his boy toy. Nodding, he faces me again and speaks. "We had a little problem with your order."

Yelling at the top of my lungs, I close the distance between us by half. "I will cut this bag! Do you understand that?" In a lower, more menacing tone, I repeat, "I *will* cut this bag."

All silent with open mouth stares, they believe me.

"It's okay, Jordan." Moonshine takes the paper grocery bag from his silent partner and places it midway between us. "I got everything but the cake."

"Did I not write, 'no exceptions'? Because I think I wrote exactly that." I'm hamming this up as best I can without laughing my ass off.

It's gone on long enough that I'm not sure the others don't believe my craziness is authentic. My head is bobbing, I'm acting really excitable, and I would swear my eyes appear to be rolling inside their sockets.

His face crumples into crocodile tears. Holding his hands up to cover them, Moonshine begins defending himself as though his life depended on it. "We tried. We tried so hard." He sniffs, gaining sympathy from our onlookers. "We went to at least three twenty-four-hour convenience stores, not a cake among them."

I raise my knife one last time.

"But." He reaches for the bag while angling his body as far from my weapon as possible. "Come to Daddy," he whispers to the smooth leather case.

"Not so fast." I tuck it behind my back. "But what?"

"We found Suzy-Q's. The next best thing." He's dripping in entitlement again, sounding like I should be grateful for his inability to follow a simple command to save his precious pouch.

And he's right. Suzy-Q's are awesome. I grab the pile of deliciousness and toss him his baby.

He croons a short love song to his treasure as I rifle through my sack to be sure the rest of the order is correct.

Knowing now that this was an act and no bag was going to get cut to shreds, the trio on the platform claps generously. Moonshine takes my hand, and we both curtsy as though being presented to the queen. Moonshine adds triple air kisses thrown in the crowds' direction.

As we sit to eat and catch up, I am grateful. Not just for snack cakes, but for the best trail family a person could have.

33

JORDAN

You know that place they always reference? The one with harps and glowing light and the enveloping feeling of love? The place where when you die, you are greeted by all your loved ones who passed away before you?

Some call it Heaven. Some Enlightenment. Others Nirvana. I call it 8710 Tremont Place.

From the moment my cousin Connie burst through the front door, running at breakneck speed down her front walkway, I felt surrounded by Divine Love and acceptance. All my fears washed away, perceiving only light, airiness, and serenity.

Passed from one family member to the next, like an infant at a christening, they hugged me and kissed me and told me over and over how much I looked like my mom. Kinder words have never been expressed. Friendlier people have not existed.

They didn't even mind my stink. Someone took my pack to empty it. Another took its contents to wipe down or toss in the laundry. Connie talked a mile a minute about who was there and who had yet to arrive.

She shows me to the master bedroom and bath to allow me to

shower. She's already laid out all my new clothes, the things she's been storing for me over the last few months.

Connie leaves me to it with a kiss on the cheek and a beer in my grasp. I savor the moment as I gaze out the bedroom window and watch everyone in her backyard. Close to thirty people have arrived, with more on the way. The music is blaring, a few kids are already dancing, and everyone is merry and cheerful.

Catching my reflection in the glass, I notice my expression matches their joy. It feels impossible not to smile.

Hurrying with my ablutions, I slow down enough to luxuriate in the feeling of freshly blown dry hair. It's like a silken shawl draped across my shoulders. Even for a moment, back to being girly leaves me looking forward to the day when I can feel like this all the time.

Connie also left a dress with a note on her bed.

Dear Jordan,
I wore this little number before I had kids.
Feel free to wear it tonight if you like it.
Love, Connie xo

How could I not like it? A little black dress that, at first glance, seems a bit blah but is definitely better than hiking gear. Once I put it on, though, va-va-voom. Mid-thigh length, the hem is flirty with a ruffled edge. Spaghetti strapped, the front scoops down slightly, enhancing without slutiffying my breasts. When I turn to look at the back, I discover there isn't much of one. A thin strap angled across the bare space is all that holds it to the rest of the dress. The lightweight fabric skims over my buttocks perfectly.

After slipping into the heels she left out, I am good to go. With the warm welcome I received, I'm no longer nervous but excited to join my family in all the revelry.

Chapter 33

After hours of dancing, connecting, and sharing memories, we sit down to a buffet dinner. Once a thriving farm, Connie and her family still utilize the property as a small homestead, the food and flowers coming directly from the garden to the table.

Beneath the tent canopy, a golden glow emanates from dozens of fairy lights strung overhead, and every table is adorned with a charming centerpiece of sunflowers and mums draped over small hay bales. Electric heaters hidden in the dark corners keep us well warmed in the mountain region chill.

I sit at the head table with Connie, her husband, Hal, and their three oldest children. Hal is telling us the story of her most recent birth experience. Like everything else in their lives, it happened right here on the farm. The contractions started early in the morning when she was out milking the goats, leaving Hal just enough time to carry her to their bed before little Evan pushed his way into the world.

"Do you have anything you can't do efficiently?" I ask.

"Play golf. I get nothing but clumps of grass. Do that enough times, and they won't let you back."

"Savages," I tell her.

"That's the word they used to describe me," Connie jokes while we at the table laugh.

Interrupted by the doorbell, Connie shrugs. "Hm. I thought everyone was here." Placing her napkin on her chair, she excuses herself.

When a few minutes go by, we start to get curious. Hal decides to check on Connie simultaneous to her return with two people in tow.

"You came!" I'm up and running like a fool. Edge lifts me high off the ground and hugs me tight. I'm surprised but pleased with his response to my greeting. "You look so handsome." He's dressed in a polo shirt and slacks with a recent haircut and freshly shaved face. He looks healthy and respectable, hardly at all like my snuggle bunny friend.

I have to rub both areas. Edge's crewcut is soft like velvet, and his skin is almost as smooth. "For luck," we say at the same time. He so gets me.

When he waves to the rest of the guests, I notice the pretty lady by his side. Princess-like auburn hair tumbles down her back in loose curls, and her eyes are wide-set and dark. She's petite and curvy and smiles widely.

"Jordan, this is Wendy. Wendy, Jordan."

"I've heard so little about you! It's such a pleasure to meet you." I give her a big hug.

Wendy laughs, knowing it's a joke about her man's inability to share. "Well, I've heard a whole lot about you. The pleasure is mine." She has the sweetest sounding southern twang to her voice.

I'm about to lead them to our table when a third person exits the house.

"Adam?"

"Jordan?"

We stare at each other for what seems an eternity. *What is Adam doing here?* He looks as incongruous as running into a Starbucks on the trail. Everything goes silent around us. Even the music scratches to a halt on the record player. Edge looks prepared to fight as Wendy lays one delicate hand on his arm.

Adam shakes himself out of his surprise and says, "I-I didn't know you were here." He's nervously twisting a stack of papers in his hands. "I followed Neil. I was hoping he and I could talk." Adam keeps staring as if it's the first time he's ever seen me.

Noticing the quiet, he tells the group, "I'm sorry, folks. I didn't mean to crash your party." He looks awkward and uncomfortable, and I want him still.

My emotions battle inside me at seeing Adam again. He's as handsome as ever, and his eyes look at me so kindly, yet my resentment boils just beneath the surface. I want to plead with him to take me back, but at the same time, I want to kick his sorry ass to the curb.

Removing myself from the situation is my best course of action. I mean, Adam said it. He didn't come for me. I offer a "Good luck," unsure how his request will be received.

I walk back to my table, keeping an eye on them as I sit. I can see

Chapter 33

the muscle in Edge's jaw working furiously. Wendy stands on tiptoe to whisper something into his ear. Looking her in the eyes, she gives Edge a slight nod and a kiss on the cheek.

To my surprise, Edge relents and walks back through the house with Adam.

Connie and I busy ourselves making room for Wendy and getting her food and drink. We make extra space for Edge, and Connie insists on another place setting.

"Hey, Adam is here too. We welcome all who come in peace." She whispers to me before retaking her seat. "I don't know why, but the second I saw him, I liked him."

I don't tell her, "Me too." I don't tell her anything. I pretend to eat and engage the entire time with one eye on the patio door.

Will Edge hurt Adam? Adam may have his strong side, but Edge is a mountain of a man. And he's angry. Don't they say high emotion can make people even stronger?

It's awful sitting here and not knowing what was happening. Wendy senses it and tells me, "It's okay. Neil is in a different place. Don't worry about your friend."

I'm not sure if she's referencing Adam or Edge.

Connie tries to stop me from cleaning up, but I'm going to go cuckoo if I don't do something.

I get to hand washing the more delicate pieces of stoneware, allowing the warm, sudsy water to lull me into a state of here and now. The bouquet of the soap is intense. More potent than I recall. They say your nose can change on the trail, which makes sense. All I smell, day in a day out, is natural, organic, and often my specific odor. The scent of "clean" can be wonderful to me at times, off-putting at others.

I pull out a bunch of dessert plates to help with the last course of the meal. As I'm exiting the kitchen with my final stack, Edge comes back inside. He now holds the papers Adam had with him. Tucking them under his arm, he grabs the dishes, "Here. I'll take these. You try to catch up with Adam. He's not staying."

I have no idea what he means. Did Edge freak out? Is Adam beat to a pulp and rushing off to find a doctor? Or did he decide he wants nothing to do with me anymore? I don't know the answers to any of it, and Edge is already out the door. Having no recourse, I run.

Adam

I was stunned when I saw Jordan. Taken entirely unaware, I stood there like a bumbling fool.

Sheila found out where Neil was going to be, and I took it from there. Following him for hours, I finally cornered him at a place I thought we might have some privacy. Sixty pairs of watchful eyes begged to differ.

But I only had eyes for Jordan. Where did she get that dress? I wanted to cover her up with my jacket to hide her beauty *and* take her to the nearest bedroom to discover the rest of the lovely body she had hidden under the scant amount of fabric.

With her lips forming an O of surprise, it was all I could do not to grab her and kiss her senseless. Or kiss some sense into her. I don't know which. Doesn't she know what she does to me, to my heart?

I can't stay to find out. My flight leaves early in the morning, and I did what I came to do. Had I been better prepared, things may have gone differently.

Jordan

I'm too late to catch Adam. I run as fast as possible, throwing the heels off to hasten my pace when I hit the asphalt, but it's no use. I see taillights ahead and call out, hollering for Adam to stop, but he leaves me in the dust.

Cold without the blower from the electrical heaters to warm me, I sit in the middle of the road and sob.

When is it my turn? I want to know. When will anything work out for me?

34

JORDAN

Someone saved me a big piece of chocolate cake. I am going to find that person and thank them profusely right after I scarf it down. I look in the freezer and find a tub of vanilla ice cream to join in the festivities.

No one knows I'm back yet. It's now that quiet period when a party begins to wind down, and no one is in a hurry to leave. The murmur of voices floats through the screen door, but I no longer hear the cranking music. A simple piano melody floats through the air, calming the senses.

I'm glad for my moment alone to regroup. The sugar should help the pain, though nothing on earth can mend this broken heart. Watching Adam drive away was worse than when I split with Brett. I was disappointed but knew better things were on the horizon after the divorce. Nothing waits for me after Katahdin.

To keep my mind off negative things, I begin to wonder if I should try to triple crown. I'll still need a place to regroup. The gear I have will need replacing due to wear and the fact that what I need for the other two hikes is probably different than what I have now.

I don't know how I feel about it. Thru-hikers tend to either do one or all three U.S. hikes, so that is a real consideration. The reality is I don't have anything else. It's been me and the trail for months now. I could never go back to a nine-to-five work-a-day lifestyle. *You might as well stick with what you know.*

As I slide from the barstool to carry my dishes to the sink, the back door opens, and in walks Edge.

"Hey," I greet him.

"Did you catch him?"

Afraid I might break, I simply shake my head.

"Sorry."

I nod.

"Let's sit." He gestures to the small loveseat tucked in an intimate nook. It seems the perfect place to have your morning coffee with its large windows and views of fields outlined in stone walls.

"Adam made good on his word. I'm quite shocked and more than a little blown away. I almost told Wendy, but I wanted to show you first. Here." He hands me the stack of papers. "Get a load of this."

I read through it, forcing myself not to fall asleep. Why does every official document have to be filled with foolish words and phrases that you need to read six times to understand ten percent of it? I make myself because it is important to Edge, and it is the last thing I ever saw Adam touch. Possibly the closest I'll be to having his hands near me again.

Looking at the bank account statement to be sure it isn't a mirage, I ask, "Have you ever seen so many zeros?"

"Not since first grade, when the teacher had me tracing numbers over and over."

"Is it for real?" I'm incredulous. "Did someone slip something in the punch?"

"I said the same thing. I almost knocked his lights out for making a mockery of it all. He got me in touch with his lawyer, the banker, and his stockbroker. After that, it seemed too much work for a practical joke. I guess it's real." Edge angles his body towards me and takes my hands in his. "We've had this discussion, and I know you don't want to hear it, but Wendy is right. It's time for me to forgive and move forward. If I have to, you have to as well. It was my battle, and it's over. Thank you for fighting by my side like a true friend."

I can't hold the tears back anymore, and he pulls me close. It's a side of him I have never seen, and I ask where he's been hiding it.

"It's all Wendy. Isn't she something?"

I can't see his face with my own still buried in his chest, but I can tell he's grinning ear to ear.

"The moment I met her, there was this shift, like the world was back in full color, and I could hear the birds singing again. Even my anger and resentment started to slip away. I tried to hang on, but I can't anymore. I can have vitriol or wellbeing. I can't have both. After a while, it became a no-brainer."

"You love her." I state the obvious as I sit back up, mopping up my tears from his shirt and my face with a napkin.

"I do. I'm going to ask Wendy to marry me."

"What?" Will wonders never cease? "You said you were married to the land."

He grins and shrugs. "What can I say? People change." His expression takes on a more serious cast. "I guess now is as good a time as any to tell you."

I cover my face like a child. "Now what?" I don't know if I can stand any more revelations tonight.

"I'm officially off the trail and moving to Tennessee."

I'm crestfallen. I thought we would peak the last mountain together. We've come so far in more ways than one. "What are you going to do in Tennessee?"

"Get to know my woman better. Settle down. Probably get a dog."

"I'm jealous. But I'm also thrilled for you. You deserve every happiness in the world, my friend."

Wendy finds us hugging one last time. When I see her, I pull away and stand to leave.

Edge stops me. "Don't go. I want you here for this."

He stands and walks closer to his lady love. We both watch as he pulls a small black box out of his pants pocket. My friend came prepared.

"Wendy, I feel like I've known you forever, but every time I see you, I get the same thrill as the day we met. I never want to be without you. Will you marry me?"

His short but heartfelt speech has us all misting up. Where Edge tends to be a man of few words, the attempt is even more meaningful. They will have a long, happy life together. I know it.

Wendy whoops out a joyful, "Yes!" Edge swoops her into his arms, kissing her as though he'll never let go.

I sneak out and allow them to celebrate their beautiful moment.

※

Connie and I stay up star-gazing long after the crowd goes home. It will take me a while to process this night, and I relish the laid-back girl time.

"Well, I've never seen a man so clearly in love. Okay, one time, there was this man named Hal." Her smile is that of a woman still profoundly in love. They've been married almost twenty years and somehow make it look easy. Four kids and a farm, and they always find time to connect in small and large ways. He leaves her love notes, and she folds his laundry. He takes her away, just the two of them, every winter. She brings him breakfast in bed on random days, like a Wednesday.

"I know. You should have met him in March. You would never have believed Edge had a tender side tucked away."

He and Wendy left soon after the proposal. He still hasn't shown her the massive bank account Adam opened for him. I wish I were going to be there for that one. Edge promised to video it for me. He'd better. It's not every day you get engaged *and* become a multi-millionaire.

Connie looks at me strangely. "I'm not talking about your hiking buddy. I'm talking about Adam. I could see two tiny red hearts in his eyes when he got a look at you."

"Isn't that the signature cartoon symbol for lust?" Pepé Le Pew, that debonaire skunk, comes to mind.

"You're too caring to be so cynical. The guy loves you. Trust me. I can usually tell these things. I saw none of that when I met Brett. If you remember, I didn't even know you two were married. I thought he was your insurance salesman."

I don't know why, but I feel the need to defend my ex. "We were getting close to filing for divorce when you met him."

"Still. Did Brett love you at one point? Yeah, probably. But he's the kind of guy that cares about others within the confines of who they are at any given moment. Adam strikes me as the real deal. I say you take Edge's advice and forgive him."

"What if it isn't enough? I mean, he came here, saw me, and left. If he loved me as much as you seem to think, wouldn't he have stayed? Maybe tried to talk?"

"Would you have stayed to talk with a woman surrounded by sixty of her closest relatives when the reason you came was to eat crow for somebody else?"

"Maybe one could argue."

"You got a look at your Uncle Richard, right?"

Richard is my uncle by marriage, and I suppose he could appear intimidating if you didn't know him. Six foot five, wearing a grey suit and an apparent gun harness, it's easy to believe he is a person to be reckoned with. He looks like a prohibition-period mobster.

In actuality, he is a small-town detective with a passion for firearms and the amendment that protects the right to bear them. Every Sunday, he goes to church, has loved his wife exclusively for their entire thirty-year marriage, and raised three daughters, each making their mark on the world. He came to the party with stacks of photo albums and a thick handful of copies for me to have. Uncle Richard is generous and kind and a great hugger. But, yeah, huge.

"I suppose you have a point."

"You're darn right I do! Now, I imagine you could use a bit of sleep. Breakfast comes pretty early here, but I promise to keep the kids from bugging you until at least nine o'clock. After that, you're on your own."

Arms linked together, we head upstairs. She stops on the second floor. I'll be continuing on to the attic playroom, where a cot is set up just for me.

"Take my advice, Jordan: Go for it. You deserve to be adored by someone who truly loves you. Find out if Adam is that man. Knowing is always better than wondering."

"That sounds like something I once told a trail angel."

She hugs me good night, exasperated. "Then take your own advice and get crackin'."

"Love ya, cuz," I tell her as I mount the last few stairs.

35

JORDAN

After a teary goodbye, I left my family with a lifetime supply of well-wishes, and I'm now back at the top of Mount Washington. Dragging my feet, I sign the hiker logbook and grab myself a hot bowl of soup. The weather channel says the first frost is coming early, and they are expecting a colder than usual autumn. I hope the meteorologists are wrong, as they can tend to be.

Typical of a mountaintop, the sights here are spectacular. I can see five states as I mosey around the circumference. Trees are beginning to change into their autumn finery. I spy red, yellow, and orange clustered together like fireballs. Fall in New England is a sight to behold, especially from the summit of its tallest peak.

It's fun to watch the people. The ones who drove to the top stand out like sore thumbs. Bright-eyed and rested, they smile and laugh, oblivious to the zombie-like thru-hikers interspersed around them. That is until they get a whiff of a person who appears to be homeless. Their expressions are one of disgust while they look around as though needing to report this olfactory abuse.

The day and section hikers have the best of both worlds. They're a bit trail weary but happy with their success. They are more likely to

Chapter 35

engage with us, asking all kinds of questions, hoping that they too will accomplish this or a similarly challenging goal one day.

It's for the rack-railway people that I save all my pity. Ratcheted up the mountain one grating, clunky gear at a time, they step off the contraption a bit green around the gills. Regretting the decision to ride in this and not a smooth moving car, they begin to realize that they'll have to board again and do it backward after a short respite. It makes a person want to take up backpacking.

Soon enough, the fog begins to descend, and I know it's time to head down this mountain to reach the next. And the next. And so on, until I have peaked Katahdin.

I'm feeling every emotion under the sun. I'm happy that I'm so close to fulfilling the most outstanding achievement of my life. I'm sad because then what? I'm grumpy because I already feel so cold, and it isn't even close to nighttime. I'm glad because I can get up every day and run it the way I want.

That has been one of my favorite parts, and I have so many favorites. But little things like not having to set the alarm and not checking in with another human are so liberating. I eat when I'm hungry. I sleep when I'm tired. I sing when I feel like it or suspect bears are around. It all comes down to freedom, and freedom is my favorite.

※

I'm wearing every layer of clothing that I own, a hat and mittens included. I wrapped myself up like a burrito in my sleeping bag liner before slipping into my sleeping bag, and still, I am freezing my butt off. It's the tip of my nose. It is always the tiny little nub of tissue when the thermometer drops. The rest of me can be as warm as toast, while my nose feels like a fleshy ice cube. I take one mitten off and wrap my hand around the offending body part, hoping it heats up before my digits feel the freeze.

They weren't kidding when they said it would get cold. It's been twenty degrees during the day, even with the sun high and the brilliant sky blue. Night temps have gone as low as minus five before factoring in the windchill. Tonight is a balmy two degrees with a steady rustle through the trees. I've slept an average of four hours the past few days but have no desire to night-hike. If I thought it would make a difference, I'd take the hit, but the extended forecast shows no end in sight to the frigid weather.

I'm not very comfortable, either. Sure, I have layers and a great pad to sleep on, but I have to keep all the gear that can't hack the cold snuggled up with me. My water bottles, filter, and even the propane stove are in here to keep them from freezing and breaking. If I lost my ability to have a hot meal at this point in the hike, I would surely lose my shit.

It's quiet on this last leg of the journey. I'm making good time considering the weather. I slip and slide a lot more now, with many narrow waterways already partially or entirely frozen. With less than a hundred miles left, I know I've got this, but I miss running into people. I read all the updates but somehow keep missing my buddies. Some have already finished, and others left the trail to help Katydid. She slipped off a short ledge, slamming her skull into a sharp rock. The two guys hiking with her had to fashion an emergency rescue sled using their hiking poles and tents to get her to the road, where an ambulance met them. Word has it that she should be okay but will not complete the hike this go around. As for her friends' finishing, no one seems sure. Knowing her, if she's conscious, I bet she's been working on kicking them out. Thru-hikers support each other, and quitting isn't an option, barring a massive head wound or another catastrophic event.

I know others must be hiking behind me, and I wish they would catch up. Something about the colder weather makes everything around me seem so desolate and lonely. Even though the sun shines bright above, with all the layers I need to keep from dying of exposure, I'm not getting the feel-good vibe the sun tends to give other times of the year with its bounty of essential vitamin D.

I revel in a sit-down lunch consisting of a bagel with cream cheese and a bag of potato chips. It's not healthy, but it will fill the void until I can get more substantial vittles. I torture myself for a time, thinking

Chapter 35

of all the yummy treats waiting for me at the end of the trail: salad, broccoli, a hot, fresh-from-the-oven baked potato with butter, sour cream, and chives. I can imagine the fat coating my tongue; it feels so good. Lately, my cravings are primarily healthy, even if my daily fare isn't.

As I pack up, I see my first flake. *Darn.* Autumn appears to have just segued into winter.

※

The snow is as relentless as the wind. Since the first flake, it has remained falling both day and night. It doesn't accumulate too much, maybe two inches at most per twenty-four-hour period, but without a lot of melting, it's building up steadily.

I focus on every step to avoid injury. This white stuff is a challenge I was hoping to avoid, though getting to the top of this final mountain was never going to be easy. It's so freakin' high, and I'm exhausted. I just didn't think it would snow so soon, especially not this amount. Even with my planned zeros, I let myself believe I left early enough to avoid it all. Stupid in retrospect. The weather shift may be unexpected, but such is the mercurial nature of a mountain.

I will be reaching the summit alone tomorrow. No one has caught up. Katydid headed for home after they discharged her from the hospital, and her saviors are miles behind. All the people I expected to come and celebrate my victory have bailed. I spoke with them individually and can't blame them one bit. It won't be safe.

A blizzard will be arriving tomorrow afternoon to add to the many inches of snow already testing my winter boots. I should peak shortly after sunrise and need the extra time to find my way to the hotel. Having no cell service right now, I can't order a ride until I do.

At least I won't be homeless when I reach rock bottom. (Ha! It's heartening that even though I'm freezing, I can still pun.) Edge has offered me the use of his and Wendy's house as they will be wintering in Tahiti. La-di-da. I only begrudge him his new lifestyle of the rich and not-so-famous a ton, but we won't let it come between us.

Connie tells me her attic cot is ready and waiting for me to come back.

Then there's Adam. He still wants me in his life and claims to be willing to give me anything, now even the moon and stars, when he can afford a trip to space. He's offered his place to me as well.

I haven't answered any of them. Edge's offer comes with an addendum: I would be living with Wendy's older brother. "He's super nice," they tell me. It sounds super awkward, and therein lies the problem. Connie is lovely and gracious, but she's not wrong. Those kids get up early. I may want to sleep in for a short while once I finish.

Would I love to stay with Adam? Yes! However, though positive, our conversations have been clumsy and shy, like two newborn foals trying to find our footing. I think all we need is time. Unfortunately, being hours away from running out of time to make up my mind, I don't know that he is an option either.

I set up my tent, knowing it's the last official camp out of my journey. It seems crucial to experience every move as I thread the tentpoles, set up the bedding, grab my dinner supplies, and take care of my pack.

36

JORDAN

Not injury nor heartbreak stopped me. My ex-husband, with his ulterior motives, didn't stop me. Falling in love with Adam didn't stop me. I am one hundred feet away from the peak, and nothing on earth can prevent me from succeeding. I count my footfalls, ignore the charley horse that trotted into my thigh two days ago and still has yet to release, and finally reach the summit of Mount Katahdin.

The tears began falling long before now. If anyone else were around, I'd blame the biting wind, the frigid cold, and the snowflakes increasing their intensity, but they would all be lies. I'm so happy and somewhat sad, and everything feels dream-like, as though none of this actually happened.

But it did. Half covered in snow and ice, the sandwich board stands there, claiming my arrival and advertising my success. I wipe away what I can and fall to my knees, spreading my arms across its breadth. Kissing the sign soundly, I rub my nose with my mitten and push myself up to my feet. All I see is snow and blur when I turn full circle with arms held high in a champion stance. But I know it is all there, all my trials, all my successes, every last bit. Pulling out my cell phone, I snap a couple of photos of the board to document that I actually and truly made it.

Someone left a small mason jar hanging on a string. I look inside and, a miracle of miracles, find my plastic shamrock. I'll probably never know who took it, but I forgive them immediately.

I'm not alone, after all. My mother is here to celebrate my success with me.

"Thanks, Mom. I love you so much." I press the medallion close to my heart before tucking it safely into my zippered pocket.

I turn to make my way down the mountain, hoping cell service will soon follow when a figure appears out of the gloom.

"Where is everyone?" He looks like Nanook of the north in all his winter garb.

"They bailed. It wasn't safe."

"This isn't safe for you either. I had to come and see for myself that you were okay."

"I'm better now that I don't have to do this by myself."

Pushing off the hood of his parka, Adam removes my pack and wraps his arms around me, pulling me as close as possible. "Did you honestly think I'd let you do that?" Before I can answer, he's kissing me. "May I be the first to congratulate you?" he whispers, caressing my lips with his words.

Oh, wow. I really have missed his mind-blowing kisses. I whisper back, "I think you're already doing that." I deepen the kiss as I savor the cold, crisp taste of an outdoor man. This man. My man.

The snow continues to fall, but neither of us cares. Impervious to the cold air swirling around us, we continue to kiss for a while. It's been so long since I've felt Adam's loving touch, his sexy mouth on mine.

Pulling away, at last, he steps back but still holds onto me. "We need to get you off this mountain, but first…" He drops to one knee.

I can't believe this! To go from feeling alone and separated from those I love, now juxtaposed with having all I want kneeling right in front of me, is more surreal than knowing I succeeded.

Chapter 36

Adam holds up a small box and opens it so I can see what is inside. "Jordan, will you hike the Pacific Coast Trail with me?"

"Oh my, yes!" I answer him as happy as a bride on her wedding day. Tears of joy stream down my cheeks. He's here, and we're good. I am blessed. "My coordinates bracelet. Where did you find it?" I push up my sleeve to help him sit it just so on my wrist. He adjusts the solid gold toggles to keep it snug and kisses my palm tenderly before covering everything back up.

"You left it at the hotel in Massachusetts."

"I'm so glad. I had no idea what happened to it. I thought it was gone forever."

He gently dries my cheeks with his palms. His touch warms me in a way no blazing fire or subzero sleeping bag ever could. "I would have bought you a new one if that was the case. I'm glad you left it too. It became my talisman. I would look at it whenever things between us felt hopeless. Your goal was to crest Katahdin. Mine was to prove I was worthy enough to have you by the time you got here."

"Oh, Adam." I hug him close. "I love you so much."

"And I love you, Jordan."

A gale-force wind interrupts our moment and nearly sweeps us off our feet.

"We need to get out of here!" Adam hollers. "Come on, give that to me." He takes my pack, pretending it's too heavy for him to lift, before making proper adjustments to sling it over his back.

"You're coming home with me, Jordan. But be warned: I'm never going to let you go."

"I'm never going to let you."

EPILOGUE
JORDAN

Hot and sweaty, Adam and I drag ourselves up to Kennedy Meadows General Store, the Gateway to the Sierra Nevada Mountains, where people sit under shade trees cheering and clapping for us. We made it through the desert. Our first significant PCT accomplishment is sweet.

Adam takes me by the hand, grinning broadly. I'm so proud of him. It's his first official accolade for being a thru-hiker. Not to say that I haven't been a special sort of cheerleader, but those details are shared just between the two of us.

Honestly, I didn't believe he was serious when he made his proposal. I thought he had simply come up with an ingenious way for the boy to get the girl. I had to say yes because one, I was already ninety percent sold on the idea, and two, he earned major points for learning to speak directly to my heart and soul. Like Edge, Adam gets me in a way few others in this lifetime have.

When we left the mountaintop that stormy day, life slowed to a snail's pace. Snowed in at the hotel a week past our scheduled stay, we had no complaints. It was often too dangerous to do much outdoors, so we filled our time loving each other and planning for our future.

Epilogue

Once we left, time began to fly again. Adam still had a few details to address regarding leaving his position, and I had lots to research for our endeavor. So many things to purchase, especially now that I was buying for two—hikers, that is. I scrutinized maps, downloaded apps onto our phones, and purchased the necessary permits. The to-do list for both of us seemed endless. Lots of work, but all for our benefit, so all good.

It's been quite a while since I've received any poems, appropriated or not. Brett showed up long enough to take his share in his second divorce before disappearing again. My stepsister remains with her daughter's birth father, and I find myself wishing them nothing but the best from afar.

Getting a divorce became a no-brainer for Kim once she realized the depth of Jonathan's deception. The constant cheating took a backseat to his embezzling ways, and she testified against him in court. Adam and I sat beside her as Jonathan was led away to prison in cuffs. It was a beautiful sight to behold! In a petty attempt at retaliation, Jonathan signed over all parental rights of Liam. A blessing, indeed! And not only because Jonathan will be spending the next few years behind bars, but because Jonathan is a dick.

Kim and Liam live in Adam's house while we "walk the world," as Adam puts it. (He's a bit of a dramatic hiker. Not quite Moonshine level, but still next level.) Kim had no reason to look for housing when we wouldn't be using it. She's turned it into a B&B, mainly focusing on the thru-hiker population. It seemed a no-brainer. I had a great time when I stayed, and the initial online reviews are in agreement.

The months we were all living together, planning and strategizing our dreams, Adam became a fabulous filler-dad. It is the most gratifying thing to watch him bond with my friend's little cherub. They play No-See-Um Liam, their unique version of peekaboo, obsessively. We have to do it over the phone these days, but he giggles and squeals with the same amount of zeal. We'll be taking two zeros to visit with both mom and baby for real, starting tonight. My arms have been itching to hold him for days.

It's made me yearn to have my own child again. I know it's not possible biologically, but Adam says we can do whatever I want as far as options. He tells me almost nightly he is willing to make the ultimate sacrifice and, "End this thru-hike right now!" if I decide to pursue a dream off-trail. He's always angling, but I do believe the hiker lifestyle is seeping under his skin.

Edge and Wendy are still traveling the globe, but not on foot. A master of many skills, Edge has a captain's license, and they spend their days yachting from port to port. He sends us a postcard at every stop, the latest in the Baltic Sea at the Port of Klaipeda in Lithuania. An obscure choice, no doubt, but he has distant relatives he wants to locate. If anyone can track them down, my snuggle bunny can.

And, yes, I said "us." Although Edge and Adam will never be what you would call friends, Jonathan's guilty verdict created an unbreakable link between the two men as their testimonies were crucial for Jonathan's sentence. That, along with Wendy's and my influence, they are cordial and polite and can stand to be in the same space for short periods, leaving us some hope for the future.

Oh! I almost forgot. Before we left the top of Mount Katahdin, Adam had one more thing to show me. He stopped abruptly, saying, "You'll need this." Removing my pack from his back, he began patting his many pockets. "Ah. There it is." Looking me straight in the eyes, he kept whatever he had found tucked behind him. "You are the most wonderful woman I have ever known. Funny, loving, adaptable, and sexy as all get out, and I would be a terrible suitor if I failed to ask you this question."

"What?" I *knew* he forgot to mention the Continental Divide Trail in his hiking scheme.

"Will you become my wife and let me love you for all time?"

My tears over the coordinates bracelet were nothing compared to the ones I shed at his proposal. I didn't even need to see the ring to know my answer was, "Oh my, yes!"

They say you can have everything you want, just not at the same time. I suppose it's true. But as I sit down with the love of my life, surrounded by all these like-minded individuals, with a plate of hot, yummy lasagna in front of me, I can't possibly imagine needing anything else.

Well, maybe that piece of chocolate cake Adam somehow conjured up.

The End

THANK YOU READERS

Thank you for reading *Trail of the Heart*! I hope you enjoyed Jordan and Adam's Appalachian Trail adventure. It would mean the world if you took a moment to post a review on Amazon and let others know your thoughts. Please visit kathleenpendoley.com, Facebook, or Goodreads for new releases, blog posts, and more information.

~ Kathleen

ACKNOWLEDGMENTS

I had so much help bringing *Trail of the Heart* to fruition. First, my heartfelt gratitude to my husband for gifting a laptop, enabling my stories to escape the confines of my mind.

My beta readers, Mary Kendzierski, Elaine Bradley, and Kait Johnson, thank you for reading through the quagmire that was my pre-edited story. Your input and support are a treasure.

I am so grateful for the many friends and family who hosted me throughout the years with open arms and giving hearts. You laid the groundwork for the hospitable atmosphere incorporated throughout the story.

I'm indebted to the following professionals: Jamie Ross of Fat Cat Design. I'm not worthy of your talent, patience, and compassion, but I am grateful. Andrew Lederman at Drew Lederman Photography, you discover beauty wherever you angle your lens. And, Author Malia Ann Haberman, thank you for recognizing my needs and sharing your gifts.

To all the dogs I've walked with, talked to, and shared my ideas first. Your ever-present Yes! to all things taught me to find the courage to go for it.

And finally, to my family, I send love and appreciation for being on my own trail of the heart.

xo

Kathleen

Made in the USA
Coppell, TX
13 July 2024